YOU WILL COME BACK

Winner of Mayhaven's Award for Children's Fiction

Terri A. DeMitchell

Terri A. DeMitchell

YOU WILL COME BACK

Winner of Mayhaven's Award for Children's Fiction

Terri A. DeMitchell

Mayhaven Publishing

Mayhaven Publishing
P O Box 557
Mahomet, IL 61853
USA

Cover Design by Aaron Porter
Original Photos by Aaron Porter & Harry Wenzel
First Edition—First Printing 2004
1 2 3 4 5 6 7 8 9 10
LOC: 2004114223
ISBN 1-932278-02-8
Printed in Canada

Dedication

To my husband, Todd, and to my parents, Bill and Rose.

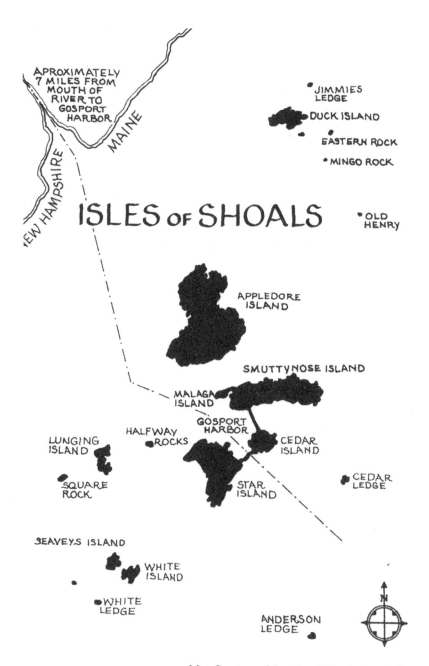

APROXIMATELY
7 MILES FROM
MOUTH OF
RIVER TO
GOSPORT
HARBOR

MAINE

NEW HAMPSHIRE

ISLES of SHOALS

JIMMIES
LEDGE

DUCK ISLAND

EASTERN ROCK

MINGO ROCK

OLD
HENRY

APPLEDORE
ISLAND

SMUTTYNOSE ISLAND

MALAGA
ISLAND

GOSPORT
HARBOR

HALFWAY
ROCKS

LUNGING
ISLAND

CEDAR
ISLAND

CEDAR
LEDGE

SQUARE
ROCK

STAR
ISLAND

SEAVEYS ISLAND

WHITE
ISLAND

WHITE
LEDGE

ANDERSON
LEDGE

N

Map Courtesy of the Isles of Shoals Association
Boston, Massachusetts

Preface

The Isles of Shoals is a group of islands located off the coasts of New Hampshire and Maine. John Smith, from the Jamestown settlement, discovered these islands in 1614. Smith originally named the islands after himself, but the name was later changed to the Isles of Shoals. Some say the name refers to the shoals (schools) of fish that were found near the islands. Regardless, in the early 1700's, some pirates took shelter at the Isles of Shoals.

Author's Note: The Isles of Shoals and its history are real. However, Olde Locke Beach and its residents are not.

Chapter One

The chocolate-colored lab barked repeatedly and strained against the dog leash as she neared the pounding Atlantic surf. Rachel held tightly to the other end of the leash until she and the panting dog cleared the side of the Isles View Hotel. As they rounded the corner, voices startled her. She hadn't expected guests would be using the beach this early in the season, especially in the morning with the wind blowing so fiercely.

"Mom! We want to stay at the beach. You said we could spend the whole day," a mousy-brown haired girl in her mid-teens complained. Another girl, slightly younger and with blond curls, joined in immediately, "I don't want to go to breakfast, I'm not hungry."

The family climbed into a van as Rachel allowed Greta to pull her closer to the beach. Greta's leash tangled the legs of a middle-aged balding man wearing purple shorts and a loud Hawaiian shirt.

"Oh, sorry," Rachel managed to say as the man almost fell to the ground. He glared at Rachel as she pulled Greta away.

They reached the white sand and Rachel unhooked the leash from the dog's collar. The lab never looked back as she tore across the sorry-looking lawn that separated the hotel from the sandy beach and surf beyond. The wind gusted and blew Rachel's long dark hair straight out behind her. She cupped her hands around her mouth and called in to the wind: "Will!" She called again. "Hey Will!"

"Behind you," a small voice said.

Startled, Rachel jumped and spun around to face her friend. "Dope!" She shoved him. "I didn't hear you sneak up behind me."

Will, holding a big rake, grinned. "Sneak? I didn't have to sneak. With the wind howling and the surf crashing, I knew you'd never hear me."

She smiled as she looked out toward the churning sea. Rachel Clark stood about an inch taller than sandy-haired Will Reynolds. They became friends in the second grade while lost on a school field trip. Now, after just completing the sixth grade, they had started a business together that included both pet and yard care. Working at the Isles View Hotel was one of their new jobs.

Business had been booming, but Rachel was worried. Will's mother, a financial planner, had been transferred to California a few weeks earlier and she wanted Will to join her. This was not part of Rachel's plan for a good summer.

She looked at the lawn that spread from the hotel to the sand. "This grass is going to need a lot of work."

Will glared at her playfully. "I had only planned on cutting the grass, not raking up half of the Atlantic Ocean's sand and rocks off of it first."

Rachel stifled a smile. A storm had hit the day before, and it had been a big one. The storm had churned up the surf and brought in a large amount of seaweed and rocks from the bottom of the ocean and scattered them all over the lawn. Rachel bent down and picked up a rock that lay at her feet and threw it out towards the water. "Well, think of it this way," she remained positive, "we'll make more money."

Will's mouth dropped open. "No, we won't. Don't you remember? We're not being paid by the hour for this job. We're being paid a flat rate."

Rachel groaned. "Whose bright idea was that?"

Will glared at her again, but this time it was less playful. "Yours!"

"Oops, that's right," Rachel said sheepishly.

It was true. The Isles View Hotel had just opened for the season. It was a small, three-story, no frills hotel. There was nothing special about it except that it had a small private beach, a great view of the Isles of Shoals, and the room rates were modest. Rachel had talked to the owners, Ben and Barb Simmons, about three weeks before about the job. A flat rate seemed like a good idea at the time.

"Maybe Ben or Barb will feel sorry for us and pay us more to clean this place up," Rachel said hopefully.

"Not likely," Will muttered.

Rachel scanned the beach. It had been deserted when she arrived. The only people she had seen were the two complaining girls with their mother and the man Greta had tangled up. Now, two teenaged boys rounded the building. They staked out their territory right in the middle of the sand and dropped their gear. A young woman, wearing a big, floppy sun hat followed them. Rachel thought for a moment that the young woman was with the boys, but she moved to the sand area farthest away from Rachel and Will.

"I'm surprised anyone is here this morning, given this wind," Rachel remarked.

Rachel looked back toward the hotel. A lone man, probably in his 30's and very fair, stood watching them. He turned away when Rachel's eyes met his. He was dressed in khakis and a long sleeved shirt. Certainly not beach attire, Rachel thought.

"What are you doing here?" Will interrupted her thoughts. "I didn't think you'd be over until later."

"I can help for a while, but I have to get Greta back soon."

Greta was one of Rachel's favorite jobs. The big, friendly dog was easy to care for. Greta loved the beach. She entertained herself and Rachel never had to worry about her running away as long as they were by the water.

The sky was clear blue. All of the clouds had been blown away by the storm. Rachel always loved the start of the summer season. Olde Locke Beach, where they lived, was a seasonal resort community. The start of summer was like a new beginning. It reminded her of starting a new year at school, but more fun. There would be new people to meet and new things to do. She knew it would be a great summer. That is, if Will stuck around to enjoy it with her.

"I ran into Mrs. Jacques who manages the apartment building. She asked if we were interested in doing gardening and mowing for her." Rachel paused for a moment to see if Will would volunteer a response. No such luck, he just began raking, so she continued, "I told her I'd have to check with you first." She paused again. "Since, you know, I can't handle the work by myself."

Will still said nothing.

Rachel waited for a moment and watched Will rake. His silence was annoying even though she knew he didn't want to talk about whether he would have to go to California. She didn't want to push, but she needed to know. The words came out of her mouth a little sharper than what she intended. "So, what should I tell her?"

Will stopped raking, but stared down at the pile of seaweed. "I probably won't be around for the job." As soon as the words left his mouth he looked up at Rachel uneasily. "Mom wants me to visit her."

"What!" Rachel's stomach did a flip. This is what she had been dreading since school had ended. Thoughts raced through her head and none of them were good. Was this just a trip? How long would he be gone? What if he liked it in California?

"When?" She almost choked on the word.

"I don't know for sure." His eyes didn't meet hers.

Rachel tried to remain calm. "How long will you be gone?"

Will again stared at the pile of seaweed at his feet and shrugged.

Rachel's attempt to remain calm failed. "Tell her you won't go!"

His eyes now met hers. "Rachel, I have to go."

"Why?" Rachel placed her hands on her hips. "Just

because your parents say you have to go?"

"No." Will crossed his arms over his chest. "I want to see her."

Rachel dropped her hands from her hips and sucked in a deep breath. She let it out slowly. That wasn't the answer she wanted. She understood. She would miss her mom, too. Rachel didn't know how to explain all her mixed-up feelings to him. Instead, she told him, "I'm leaving!"

Will's shoulders sagged. "Rachel, don't be mad."

"Why?" she demanded to know, but didn't wait for an answer. "Greta! Greta!" Rachel shouted into the wind. Greta didn't hear, or didn't pay any attention.

"Because," he argued, "I'm not leaving because I want to go away. I'm leaving because I want to see my mom."

Rachel hesitated. She knew it wasn't his fault, but that didn't make her feel any better. She was mad. It wasn't fair.

She knew Will was mad too. He picked up a rock and hurled it into the sea. Greta ran down the sand and plunged into the water after the rock, thinking it was a game. The dog barked like crazy as she thrashed in the waves trying to find it. Rachel started toward Greta. "I'm leaving anyway," she told him again, but there was less anger in her voice.

Will called to her. "Okay, leave if you want, but before you go, you'd better go out to the point. The storm brought in some traps. The tide is coming in and they could get washed away."

Rachel wanted to make a dramatic exit, but she needed to check to see if any of the traps belonged to her family. Her dad was a lobsterman and her sixteen-year-old brother worked with him during vacations. Sometimes Rachel helped too.

Rachel started out across the lawn down toward the point that jutted out into the water. This point created the Isles View Hotel's private beach at one end. The surrounding rocks were too large to allow beachgoers to wander further down the shore. Rocks at the other end of the beach formed the other barrier.

She was still deep in thought about Will when she approached the point. But, something caught the corner of her eye, a slight movement in the rocks, a flash of white and a swirl of yellow. For a moment, she thought she saw a person, perhaps a woman. Rachel blinked and looked again. Nothing.

It was then that she saw a mangled group of lobster traps stuck amid the rocks and groaned. Storms often dislodged lobster traps in the area. When lobstermen know a severe storm is coming, they remove the traps from the water.

She walked closer to the traps to check the identification. All traps must have the owner's lobster fishing license number on them. If the buoys were still attached, it would be easy to quickly identify her family's traps. Trap buoys are painted a unique set of colors so fishermen don't pull up another person's trap.

When Rachel reached the point, she saw there were only four traps, but they were a mass of wire. The lines were tangled and crossed. She climbed along the end of the rock formation until she reached the traps. The doors on two traps were open. The doors were closed on the other two. One trap was empty, but the other trap imprisoned two dead lobsters. She groaned again.

Rachel tried to untangle the traps. This was going to be a chore if these traps belonged to her dad and brother. The buoys were missing so she looked for the tags. None of the traps belonged to her family.

She was just about to climb back over the rocks to the sandy beach when she noticed a thin leather strap sticking out of the sand. She pulled on the end of the strap and a small leather pouch slid easily through the sand. At the top of the palm-sized pouch was a drawstring that cinched the opening. She spread the opening and peered inside.

Rachel gasped. She turned the pouch over and let the contents spill into her hand. "Oh my gosh!"

She clamped her hand over her mouth almost dropping the pouch, catching herself before she shouted. She looked around. The two teenaged boys were still on the beach. So was the young woman wearing the big hat. The woman now stood at the edge of the sand pointing a camera toward the surf. No one was looking at Rachel, but she could feel her heart pounding.

She had to remain calm, she told herself. She didn't want to attract attention. She pushed the contents back into the pouch and turned toward the hotel.

Rachel clutched the pouch in one hand and scrambled over the rocks, slipping once and banging her shin as her foot slipped between two boulders. She winced, but immediately pulled her foot out and kept going. One step later the pain was forgotten. Rachel reached the sand and ran full speed to Will, forgetting all about her plan to avoid drawing attention to herself.

She was completely out of breath when she reached Will. Rachel wasn't sure if it was because she had run halfway across the beach or because she was about to burst with the news.

Will had his back to her. She grabbed his arm and spun him around. "Will!" She held out her hand and dumped the contents of the pouch into her open palm.

Will's eyes and mouth flew open as he dropped the rake. "Whoa!" he exclaimed.

In Rachel's hand were four very old coins. There were three silver ones and one that looked like gold.

Chapter Two

Rachel's hand started shaking so hard the coins scattered to the ground. They both dropped to their knees at the same time, knocking their heads together as they reached for the coins.

"Who? What? Where did you get these?" Will demanded as he rubbed his head. He picked up two coins and Rachel picked up the other two.

Rachel ignored her aching head and just stared at the coins she held in her hand.

"Rachel!" Will insisted again, "Where did you find these?"

"Over...over there...over by the rocks...over by the traps...." The words tumbled over one another.

"Are there more?" Will asked as he jumped up from the sand spraying granules all over Rachel. He took off running before she had a chance to answer him.

By the time Rachel caught up with Will, he was already thrashing through the lobster traps. She saw two coins laying next to him on the sand. "Will, by your foot…coins!" Rachel shouted at him.

"Where?" Will spun around to look by his feet. He gave her an exasperated look. "Those are the two coins I already had in my hands!"

"Oh." The waves lapped dangerously close. Rachel picked them up. She placed all the coins back into the leather pouch and closed it with the drawstring. She clutched the pouch.

"Will, don't just throw the traps back into the surf!" she complained.

"Why? Were they in the traps?" Will asked, but Rachel didn't have a chance to answer him before he fired the next questions at her. "Did you dig for them? Did they wash ashore when you were just standing here?"

"No," she answered.

He stopped long enough to look at her. "No to all of the above?"

"They were in this pouch!" Rachel practically shouted the words. "And the pouch was just sort of sticking out of the sand."

"Where?"

"There." She pointed to the spot.

Will pounced onto the sand where she pointed and started digging with his hands. "Did you dig around to see if there were more?"

"No! I just ran over to show you!"

Will had already dug a hole up to his elbows, and he was going deeper.

Rachel looked back toward the beach. The boys and the young woman wearing the hat were now watching them. *Staring* at them was more accurate. Also watching was the fair man in khaki pants Rachel had seen watching them earlier.

"Will! People are watching us! I don't want them to know what we're doing."

Will didn't stop. Rachel wondered if he'd even heard her. "Will!"

Suddenly, Greta bounded up to them barking like crazy. She started digging next to Will.

"Will," Rachel said again.

"I don't care!" he said. He had heard her after all. "Besides, they don't know what we're doing." Will dug frantically. "Help me look before everything gets washed away."

Will was right. If they didn't act immediately, the changing tide would wash away anything that was there. That is, if anything else *was* there.

"Greta! Be quiet!" Rachel urged. It didn't help.

Greta dug faster than Will. Sand sprayed everywhere. Greta dug her nose into the sand.

"Did you find something, girl?" Will asked Greta hopefully.

Greta leaned back on her haunches and barked into the hole. Then she started digging again.

"What is it, Greta?" Rachel asked. "What did you find?"

Suddenly, a crab emerged from the sand. Greta lunged for it, but the crab was faster. With Greta in hot pursuit, the crab escaped into the surf. Greta bounded into the water after it, barking loudly.

"Greta!" Rachel called after her. Greta barked several more times at the surf then returned to the sand. She shook the salt water from her fur all over Rachel and Will.

"Oh, Greta!" Rachel complained as she tried to wipe the water from her face.

"Hey! That's a great idea!" Will shouted. Before Rachel could ask what he meant, Will was on his feet. Rachel watched as he ran to the gardening shed. Greta took off again as well. This time she started chasing gulls that had landed at the other end of the private beach.

Will ran back and dropped his flippers and snorkel onto the beach. He plopped down on the sand and struggled to put on his right flipper. "I'll go into the water since I have the gear. If this pouch washed up, there may be more coins below."

"We can both go down together," Rachel said. "I'm wearing my bathing suit under my clothes."

"No," he argued. "We'll only get in each other's way and stir up the sand so we can't see anything."

"The sand is already churned up," Rachel countered.

"You don't have your mask." Will tapped the one on top of his head.

Will had brought his gear that morning so he could go swimming at the private beach after he'd finished working. Ben had said it was okay since they were working there. Rachel hadn't planned on staying.

"But..." she started to argue with him.

"Hey!" The lady in the big hat yelled towards them. "You kids! Get your dog!"

Rachel had been so caught up arguing with Will that she had completely forgotten about Greta. Greta had something brightly colored in her mouth and was dragging it through the sand. It was a beach towel. The woman chased after her.

"Oh, no!" Rachel called out, "Greta! Come here girl!"

As usual, Greta paid no attention. She thought it was a game. The young woman was now screaming at Greta as the two of them ran in circles on the beach. "Come here, dog! Give that back! That's my towel, dog!"

Rachel looked at Will for help. He was now at the water's

edge. Will looked back at Rachel, shrugged his shoulders and placed his mask over his face. In an instant, he was gone.

Rachel kicked at the sand. She should have brought her gear. She kicked the sand one more time, slipped the pouch of coins into her pocket, and then took off after Greta.

Fortunately, Greta tired of the game quickly. She finally dropped the towel and ran over to Rachel. Rachel immediately grabbed her collar. "Come on Greta. You can help me."

They started walking back toward the point. The lady with the hat shouted, "Keep your dog away from me!" Rachel didn't turn around to acknowledge the woman, but she made sure she didn't let go of Greta.

She climbed back over the rock formation and began combing the crevices that spotted the rocks. Will was worried the tide would carry away any coins that were on the beach, but it was also possible the rising tide could bring in more coins. If it did, she was determined to find them.

Rachel watched Will dive with his snorkel. Every time he came to the surface after a quick dive she looked over to see if he found anything. She knew if he did, there would be no doubt.

The process of combing the crevices was slow. She started at one end and worked her way up and then down. Rachel figured, if she searched in a pattern, she wouldn't miss anything.

She only hoped Will was as organized in his search.

Rachel looked back at the teenaged boys. They looked enough alike to be brothers. Both were tall and thin with light brown hair. She figured them to be about fifteen and sixteen. Rachel had kept an eye on them because they kept moving around. During the short time since she had been there, they had thrown a football, tossed a Frisbee, and they were now splashing into the water.

They entered the water away from the place Will was diving, but were slowly moving in his direction. She wanted to shout to Will to warn him about the boys, but he already knew.

"Hey, I'm swimming here," Rachel heard Will complain as the boys came too close.

"Free ocean!" one retorted. The other laughed.

Will treaded water, keeping his eyes on the boys. Suddenly, the boys separated. One of them dove right under Will. At first, Rachel wasn't sure where the boy had gone. Then, she watched Will go under. Will sputtered as he reached the surface. He hadn't been prepared. He hadn't held his breath. Suddenly, the other boy dove down. Will sucked in a mouthful of air just as he was once again jerked underwater.

"Hey kid, you shouldn't be out here if you can't swim," one of them jeered.

"Leave me alone or..." Will barely managed to cough out the words.

"Will!" A loud voice shouted from the beach. It was Ben. Even though she knew Ben would be angry that they were not working, Rachel was really happy to see him. She was afraid Will might try to get into a fight with the teens. They were much older and bigger than he was. Will was pretty reasonable most of the time, but he could get hotheaded, especially when someone tried to bully him. "Will, get out of the water! Now!" Ben shouted.

Will swam rapidly to the shore where Rachel was searching as the boys continued jeering. When Will reached the beach he threw his gear onto the sand. "What a couple of jerks!" he said.

The two boys were now horsing around in the waves where Will had been diving.

Rachel straightened up and watched. Suddenly one of them dove down under the water, right where Will had been.

"Will! Look!"

Then, the second boy dove under.

The boys stayed underwater for what seemed to be an eternity, then surfaced together.

One of the boys shouted, "Jason! Jason! Look what I found!"

The two boys now bobbed together sharing their find.

Suddenly, a shadow moved over Rachel and Will and a voice boomed from above, "What are you two doing?"

They spun around to see Ben standing over them with his hands on his hips.

Will stammered, "Uh, you...you said we could use the beach."

Ben was a large man, probably six foot four inches.

"I said you could use the beach after you finished the cleanup." Ben's voice continued to boom. Rachel hadn't heard him enough to know if he was shouting at them or whether he was using his regular voice.

"We were just taking a break," Rachel explained.

Ben folded his arms across his muscular chest. "A break?" Ben repeated. "How can you take a break when you haven't started to work? It doesn't look like you've done a thing!"

Rachel looked over at Will.

Will jumped in. "We're sorry, but we just found..."

Before he could spill the beans, Rachel threw an elbow directly into Will's rib cage. "Ouch!"

"We'll get on it right now," Rachel told him as Will tried to catch his breath.

Ben didn't seem to notice she had just attacked Will for no apparent reason. He was too busy being angry to pay any real attention to them.

A blood vessel stuck out on the side of Ben's neck as he spoke. "Look around. Guests are starting to come to the hotel and they expect a lawn they can use—not a pile of rocks!"

"Right," Will said while rubbing his side. Rachel bobbed her head up and down.

Will started for the storage shed and Rachel started to follow.

"Hey!" Ben shouted again. "Get that dog out of here."

Rachel looked over at Will and said, "Okay, I was just…"

"Now!" Ben was clear.

Will tried to keep them together. "Let me help…" Will started to say, but Ben cut him off.

"You get to work," he told Will.

Will stopped dead in his tracks and stared at Rachel.

Rachel looked from Will's unsure face to Ben's angry one. She tapped her side pocket. "I'll meet you at our hangout for lunch," she told Will.

"But…" Will started to protest, but Rachel tilted her head in Ben's direction. She didn't want Ben, or anyone for that matter, to be suspicious. Fortunately, Will backed off. Rachel took one more look out at the two boys who were still diving by the rocks.

Ben followed her gaze. He shouted in an even louder

voice to the two boys, "Hey, you two kids! Stay away from the rocks! The surf's too heavy!"

Rachel watched the boys move away from the rocks, relieved that Ben had chased them away from the treasure. But, as soon as Ben turned his back and started to follow Will, she watched the teenagers go right back to the rocky area.

Chapter Three

Rachel paced back and forth outside the On The Rocks Cafe waiting for Will. The sandwich and pizza shop was located on a rocky section of the seacoast, near the large sandy beach where Rachel and Will spent much of their time.

Rachel checked her watch again. Will should have been there fifteen minutes ago.

Rachel reached into her front pocket and felt the leather pouch. She must have checked her pocket a hundred times already just to make sure it was still there. It was. But she didn't pull the pouch out. That would have to wait until she and Will were inside and far away from prying eyes.

She checked her watch again. "Where are you?" Rachel asked aloud just as two men exited the restaurant. She smiled at them when they gave her an odd look.

"Just rehearsing for a play." Rachel laughed nervously and then turned away. She checked her watch again.

Will rounded the building in a full run as Rachel paced in his direction. He plowed right into her, practically knocking her down.

"Dope!" she said as she pushed him. "Where were you?"

Sweat had beaded up on Will's face. "I got stuck talking to Ben Simmons," Will panted. "Do you have them?"

Rachel's eyes popped. "You didn't tell him, did you?"

"Of course not! Do you have them? Let me see!"

"Are you sure you didn't tell him?" Rachel eyed him closely. "You've blabbed before."

Will looked hurt. "We agreed that we wouldn't tell anyone! Let me see them!"

"Did those boys find anything else?" Rachel asked.

Will shook his head no. "They left right after you did," he told her. "For a moment I thought they were following you and I was going to go after them, but then I saw them go into the hotel." Will held out his hand. "Let me see them!"

"Did Ben pay you for the work even though we're not finished? He told me he would."

Will let out a growl, reached into his pocket and pulled out a folded piece of paper. "A check."

"Doesn't anyone pay in cash these days?" Rachel asked as

she reached for the check.

Will pulled it out of range of her hand. "I'll hang on to it," he said as he started to fold it and put it back into his pocket.

"Wait a minute," Rachel said. "I always hang on to the money." She was the treasurer. It was odd, though, because Will was the one who paid more attention to money.

"Yeah." Will agreed. "Why is that?"

Rachel knew immediately that he was really talking about the coins, but she didn't offer to share them with him. She didn't answer his question either. Some things are better ignored.

Will smiled smugly and put the check into his pocket.

"Is the check made out to both of us?" Rachel asked.

Will took the check out of his pocket and unfolded it again. His smile disappeared. "Yes."

Now Rachel smiled smugly.

Rachel and Will always shared the money they made from the business. Once a week, they used some of it to share a pizza and drinks. The rest was equally divided. Rachel was saving for a new bike and Will planned to save, save, save.

****

Rachel waited for change while Will walked over to the soda dispenser and got the drinks. Root beer for him and diet root beer for her. They were both far too excited to eat anything, but they had to order something to sit down inside the cafe. Rachel and Will met at a booth situated by a window in the far corner away from the other patrons and away from the ordering counter. Few customers ever walked by that area.

Will spoke first. "Rachel, I still don't know why you wanted to come here."

Rachel leaned back against the booth seat. "I just wanted time to think."

Will complained, "We could have thought at one of our houses and not had to buy drinks."

Rachel rolled her eyes and moved forward in her seat. "Will, your dad is home, right?"

"Yeah. So?"

"Well, my mom's home."

Will repeated himself. "Yeah. So?"

Rachel sucked in air in exasperation and huffed it out. "Will, neither place is very private. Someone would start asking questions and I don't want to answer any right now. I *can't* answer any right now."

"And this is private?"

Rachel nodded her head. "Who's going to come over here and ask us questions? We're just sitting here drinking our sodas."

Will sucked root beer through his straw. "That's true."

They both looked around the cafe. There were only a few patrons. It was still pretty early in the season. In a couple of weeks, the place would be packed at any time of day.

"Okay, you made your point. Let me see them again."

Rachel looked around cautiously once again. The owner was occupied at the counter and the few customers were busy eating and drinking coffee. No one was paying any attention to Rachel and Will.

"Okay, but don't let anyone else see them."

"I know, I know," Will said impatiently.

Rachel reached into the front pocket of her shorts and pulled out the leather pouch that held the coins. Rachel gave the bag one final squeeze and laid it down on the table between them.

They both stared at the tan leather pouch that was closed at the top by a leather drawstring. The leather was weathered and stained, probably from the salt water. But there were no distinctive marks. It just looked like an ordinary leather pouch.

Rachel said, "Maybe we should open it."

Will looked as if he was in a hypnotic trance. He nodded slowly, still staring at the pouch.

Rachel carefully pulled open the top releasing the tightened drawstrings. She turned the pouch over and the coins dropped into her hand. Rachel paused for a moment and gazed at them. She then laid the coins on the table, face side up. There were four coins and none looked like any coins they had ever seen before.

Will reached for the gold-colored coin. "Do you think this is real gold?" His eyebrows were arched about as high as Rachel had ever seen them.

Rachel shrugged. "I think, if you have to ask, it probably isn't." She leaned forward and gazed at the coin in Will's fingers. "It looks more like what a penny is made of."

"Yeah, you're right. What's a penny made out of?"

"Copper, I think."

"Oh yeah. I knew that," Will said as he placed it back on the table and picked up one of the silver coins. He turned it over and examined the other side.

Rachel picked up the copper-looking coin Will had set down. On the front of the coin was a profile of two people. Rachel wasn't sure if they were two men, two women, or one man and one woman. On the back it was dated. "Will, this coin says it's from 1694!"

"Wow!" Will said.

"Shhhh!" Rachel whispered and looked around. Fortunately, no one looked over at them.

"There's a date on mine too," Will whispered. "And,

you're not going to believe what it is!"

Rachel now looked at Will. "What?"

It was Will's turn to look around to make sure no one was paying any attention to him. "The date is 1698."

"Wow!" The word was out of Rachel's mouth before she could stop it. She covered her mouth with her left hand.

Rachel picked up another coin. "Will, this one says 1708!"

Their voices were getting louder. Rachel saw that a man at another table was now looking over at them. She stared at the man until he looked away.

Will reached for the last coin. It too was silver. "I don't see a date on this one." He turned it over and studied the other side. "It says AN 12." He handed the coin to Rachel.

Rachel studied the coin. She couldn't find anything that resembled a date either. She did notice something however, "This one says 2 Francs. That's French. Right?"

Will shrugged. "I don't know."

Rachel lined up the coins in a domino pattern on the table and said, "We have coins from 1694, 1698, 1708, and one coin without a date."

Staring at the coins, Will spoke. His voice was low. "Where do you think they came from?"

Rachel shook her head slowly from side to side as she stared at the coins on the table. She had asked herself the same question over and over since she found the coins. She didn't have a single answer. "I don't know."

"Well," Will hesitated. "I have an idea."

Rachel looked up at him. "Where do you think they came from?"

"I think it could be," he looked around and whispered, "pirate's treasure."

Rachel leaned back in the booth and laughed out loud. "Pirate's treasure. That's a good one!"

"Well, it could be." Will's face began to turn pink. "I've been thinking about it. There were pirates here a long time ago, and, these are old coins."

"Yeah, right!" Rachel laughed again. "Come on Will. Be serious."

Will picked up a silver coin and turned it over in his hand. "I'm not kidding." He looked at her and asked, "What else could they be?"

Will had her there. They were certainly not like any coins she had seen. Rachel's laugh turned into a chuckle. "Come on! You're joking, right?" She looked from the coins to Will. "I always thought that was just a story—that pirates sailed off of the coast."

Will slid forward and put his elbows on the table. "No, really! There were pirates here." He reached up and brushed his fingers through his hair. "Well, they weren't here, exactly. But, they were around here. Pirates traveled along the coast and some stayed out at the Isles of Shoals. Think about it. Where else could they have come from except for pirate treasure?"

Rachel watched Will as he leaned back in the cushioned booth. Maybe it was true. What other explanation was there? How did a leather bag of coins end up on Olde Locke Beach?

Rachel turned one of the silver coins over between her fingers. "Who was out there?" she asked.

Will leaned forward. His eyes sparkled as he whispered, "*B l a c k b e a r d.*"

Chapter Four

"We need to get to a coin collector!" Will said as they left the cafe.

The bright sun hurt Rachel's eyes and she squinted. "I think we should wait."

"Wait for what? It's the only way we'll find out what they're worth! Blackbeard's coins could be worth a fortune! We could be rich! We could be famous! We could be..."

Rachel stopped him. "Are you sure you want to sell them?"

Will looked startled. "Why not?"

Rachel shrugged. "I don't know. Besides, the coin collector could tell us what the coins are worth, but that isn't going to tell us if they belonged to Blackbeard."

"So?"

"Wouldn't the coins be more valuable if we could prove

they belonged to Blackbeard?"

"Maybe," Will admitted.

"Besides, where would we find a coin collector? There aren't any coin shops around here. We'd have to go to Boston."

It was true. Olde Locke Beach was a small town with a tourist population as large as the full-time resident population. For that reason, it was a town with few frills except those that drew out-of-town guests.

"We'd have to take a bus or the train," Rachel continued. "Besides, we need information now. Let's go to the library."

Will groaned. "But it's summer vacation!"

"We can check out a book about Blackbeard." Rachel smiled.

"I have a book at home on pirates and he's in it." Will's eyes brightened as he asked her, "Do you know why he was called Blackbeard?"

"Let me guess," Rachel answered. " Duh…because he had a black beard?"

Will grinned. "Yeah, funny! But it's because he had this great *big* jet-black beard that grew almost into his eyes. He used to twist it into pigtails that he tied with ribbons and wrapped them around his ears."

Rachel scoffed. "Sounds pretty. I thought he was supposed to be a blood-thirsty pirate."

"He was! When he went into battle, he put hemp cord under his hat and in his beard and set the cord on fire! Some say he looked like the Devil himself! He even left a woman out at the Shoals to guard his treasure and never came back for her."

"Nice guy!" Rachel concluded. "What ever happened to her?"

"She died." Will then leaned in close to her and whispered, "They say she's a ghost."

"A ghost?" Rachel felt a chill.

****

They climbed up the chipped brick steps of the Olde Locke Beach Public Library. Rachel struggled to open the heavy wooden door to the three-story brick building, as she said, "I want to keep this quiet until we know more about the coins. Besides, how do we know we can keep the coins if they do belong to Blackbeard?"

Will stopped dead in his tracks. "Well, of course we could keep them. Why couldn't we keep them? You always hear stories about people discovering treasure and getting rich."

"But, think about it, Will. If the coins belong to Blackbeard, then he probably stole them, right?"

Will shrugged. "So?"

"Well, would we have to give them back?"

Will tensed. "Rachel, you take the fun out of everything."

"I know," Rachel said as they entered the library.

The Olde Locke Beach Library was once a private home. Entering the foyer, a set of stairs was directly ahead and rooms filled with books jutted out immediately on both sides. The room to the right was once a living room and the one to the left was once a dining room. Both rooms had fireplaces that warmed the library building in the winter. Rachel enjoyed coming to the library after school during the cold months to do homework, or to just sit and read.

Mrs. Tompkins, the librarian, sat behind her desk and smiled at them as they entered. She had helped them with projects before. She was one of those great librarians who didn't hover. She helped if you asked, but left you alone the rest of the time.

Rachel and Will went to the computer bank that was against one wall. There, they could locate any book in the library. Rachel went to the subject listing and typed in the word coins.

Will went to another computer and got on the web. "We could have done this at my house," he complained. Will never liked spending a lot of time in the library, but loved using a computer.

"Shh," Rachel said. "I don't want anyone bothering us."

"Shh," Will echoed.

"What are you looking up?" Rachel asked him.

Will held his hand up for a moment to signal her to wait until he'd finished typing. "I'm searching for coins and Britannia. One of the coins said Britannia on the back." He waited for the search to come up.

Rachel walked over to him and looked over his shoulder. "Hey look. It says Great Britain. Isn't that England?"

"I think so," Will answered as he typed a new search. "I think Blackbeard was from England."

This time he searched for coins and francs. The screen flashed and revealed new information. He clicked on to the first entry. When the results came up on the screen both he and Rachel leaned forward to read them.

Rachel paused for a moment. "It's a foreign language. I'll bet it's French."

Will looked at her eagerly and asked, "Can you read it?"

Rachel let out a long sigh, placed her hands on her hips and asked, "And, just when do you think I learned French?"

"Well, I don't know."

"Will, you've known me since the second grade. During that time, have I ever taken French?"

"Okay, okay." He relented. "What did *you* find out?"

"The computer says the books on coins are in Section 737.

That's upstairs on the second floor, but we need to check on Great Britain."

Will looked around. "There's a dictionary on the table over there. Maybe it will help."

"Why Will, how low-tech," Rachel remarked, but walked to the book anyway. "Great Britain, Great Britain," she muttered as she thumbed through the pages. "Here it is. It says Great Britain is an island of Northwest Europe and it's made up of England, Scotland, and Wales."

"England!" Will smiled and then whispered loudly, "Blackbeard!" He stood up and walked over to her.

Rachel smiled back. "Let me look up 'franc' and then we can go upstairs."

Will leaned in and read the entry along with her.

"It says that the franc is the basic currency…" she turned to Will and explained, "that means money."

"I know, I know."

Rachel continued, "The franc is the basic currency of Belgium, France, and Luxembourg."

Will rubbed his fingers through his hair. "France is the only country I've heard of."

"Yeah, me too." Rachel nodded. "Let's go upstairs and see if we can find these coins."

They climbed the wide staircase and found the section. The

books were located on a top shelf. Will went to the end of the row and got a stool. He climbed up and read titles off to Rachel.

There were only six books on the subject and all but one dealt only with United States and Canadian coins. The coins in the pouch were definitely not from either country.

"Doesn't anyone want to know about foreign coins?" Will asked. He pulled the only book about world coins from the shelf and handed it down to Rachel.

She took it to a table while he put the stool back against the wall. Rachel looked at the index. The coins were listed by country. Will sat down next to her.

Rachel sighed. "This may take a while." She removed the coins from her pocket and set them on the table. There was no one on the upper floor of the library but them.

Rachel and Will began with Great Britain. Once they found the country, it wasn't hard to identify the coins because they were listed by dates.

"Look! Here's a picture of the 1694 coin with the two heads," Rachel said. "It's a copper farthing with a picture of William and Mary on the front." Rachel chuckled. "So it *is* a man and a woman."

"Who are they and what's a farthing?"

"It says here that William and Mary ruled from 1688 to 1694. I guess a farthing is what the coin's worth."

"Right," Will agreed. "It must be like a penny or a dime. I'm going to get a piece of paper and a pencil. We need to write this down."

When he returned he said, "I'll start a list."

"Let me see the book." Will slid it closer. "1694 William and Mary copper farthing."

Rachel looked at the paper. "That should be enough. We have the date, the ruler, what the coin is made of, and what it was worth. Does it say what a farthing was worth?"

Will shook his head. "No."

Will had already found the next coin and matched it to the entry in the book. He said, "1698 William III silver half crown." Then he wrote it down.

Rachel found the last British coin. "1708 Anne silver half crown."

Will wrote down the information and said, "Now go to the section on France and see if we can figure out what the date is of this coin."

Rachel flipped through the book and found France. "This is harder because we don't know the date."

Will looked over the coin, turning it in his fingers. "It says AN 12. It's kind of hard to read, the coin is pretty beat up. Oh, and it says Bonaparte."

"Bonaparte must be the ruler." Rachel guessed. "His picture's on the front of the coin."

Will wrote down Bonaparte. They spent time looking through the section on French coins. "Rachel, look!" He pointed to a small paragraph at the corner of the page. "It says, 'L'An. A special calendar used during the French Revolution.'"

Will held the coin close to his eyes. "I only see an AN. Maybe there's an L. I can't see..."

Rachel leaned over the page. "Does it give a date?"

"No, it just says that L'An 1 is for the first year of the revolution."

"So," Rachel concluded, "L'An 12 must be the twelfth year of the revolution!" She beamed. "Write that down."

Will wrote, "L'An 12 Bonaparte silver franc." He slammed the book shut. "We've got it!" He grinned back at her, but suddenly became serious. "These coins are probably valuable, I really think we should split them up."

"Or we should put them in a safe place. What about a safe deposit box at the bank?" she suggested. "We could get a box together and each have a key. That way the coins would be safe." Rachel knew her parents had a box at the bank where they keep important documents.

Will shook his head. "It won't work. You have to be eighteen to have a safe deposit box."

"How do you know?"

"I wanted to get one a couple of years ago to put some of my savings bonds and baseball cards in, but, Mom said I'd have to be eighteen to get a box, so I put the stuff in my parent's box." Will held out his hand. "Let's divide them up."

"Not here. Let's go look at your book on Blackbeard."

"Okay." Will agreed. "We can split up the coins at my house."

Rachel was just about to speak when he added, "My dad knows a lot about stuff around here. You can stay for dinner and we can ask him some questions. Without being too obvious, of course."

"Oh, Will!" she complained. "You know I don't like being around your father. He makes me feel weird."

Will nodded. "Yeah, I know. That's because he's a teacher. He makes me feel weird too when we're just talking, but if he's teaching me something, he's not that bad."

Rachel looked unsure. "But what if he gets suspicious?"

"He won't. He's too busy being mad at Mom to pay any attention to what I'm doing. Since Mom left, he's not very fun to be around."

Rachel looked at him and teased, "Will, your dad has never been very much fun to be around."

Chapter Five

Rachel placed her napkin onto her lap and waited for Will to join her and his father at the kitchen table. He couldn't get there soon enough for her.

Will's father taught fifth grade at the Olde Locke Beach Elementary School. When Rachel was in fourth grade she dreaded the thought of having Mr. Reynolds the next year. He definitely wasn't the most popular teacher. He was okay, just really strict. She had been relieved to find out she would be in Ms. Hanson's fifth grade class.

"You know, my mom is studying to be a teacher." Rachel tried to make conversation with Mr. Reynolds.

"That's what Will tells me. Is she planning on teaching elementary school?"

Rachel nodded yes.

"It's a wonderful profession."

Rachel nodded again and glared in Will's direction. She tried to send him a telepathic message to hurry up.

"Rach, you want a root beer?" Will asked as he opened the refrigerator door.

"Yeah. That'd be great."

Mr. Reynolds frowned at her.

Rachel corrected herself. "Uh…I mean yes, please."

Mr. Reynolds always had perfectly combed hair—just the opposite of Will. And he was dressed in a white, button-down collared shirt. Who wears a white shirt when eating spaghetti? Rachel looked down at her red tee shirt and smiled. A red tee shirt was the perfect attire for a red sauce. But knowing Mr. Reynolds, there wouldn't be a speck of sauce on his shirt at the end of the meal.

Will's father was mixing spaghetti with the tomato sauce. Rachel and Will had already made the salad that sat on the kitchen table.

Making the salad had not gone well. Rachel was in the middle of cutting the romaine lettuce with a knife when Mr. Reynolds told her she was supposed to tear lettuce, not cut it. And Will poured Italian dressing all over the tossed salad just before his father asked for ranch dressing on the side.

"That spaghetti smells wonderful, Mr. Reynolds," Rachel

told him. "Is that a family recipe?"

"No, I opened a jar," he said. "I'm not much of a cook."

Rachel looked hopelessly over at Will who rolled his eyes as he came to the table with two cans of root beer. He handed the diet root beer to her.

She took her can and popped the top.

"Will, get glasses for the drinks," his father instructed.

Will went to the cupboard and took out two glasses and took them to the table. Mr. Reynolds placed some spaghetti on a plate and handed it to Rachel. He then looked at Will who had just taken his seat. "Will, I'd like a glass of ice water, and perhaps your guest would like some ice for her drink as well."

Rachel shook her head no.

Will got up and got the glass of ice water and brought it to the table.

Mr. Reynolds handed a plate of spaghetti to Will. "Speaking of someone who cooks better than I do," he paused long enough for Will and Rachel to exchange quick looks over the table, "you need to call your mother."

Will gulped down the chunk of tomato he'd just placed into his mouth. "I'll call her tonight."

"Call at 5:30 her time, 8:30 our time. That's when she said she would be home from work."

Will simply nodded and quickly changed the subject. "We

did the clean-up work at the Isles View Hotel. Boy, what a mess after the storm. There were rocks and seaweed everywhere."

"Don't get too involved with your summer work," Mr. Reynolds said as he rolled spaghetti onto his fork. "You know your mother wants you to fly out for a visit."

Rachel's stomach tightened.

Will looked at her and then back to his father. Then he really changed the subject. "Dad, there were pirates around here, right? Blackbeard was here, right?"

Rachel grimaced. She would have kicked Will under the table if he had been closer. She settled for giving him a blazing glare. Rachel was certain Mr. Reynolds would start asking a lot of questions.

Fortunately, Mr. Reynolds just looked confused. "There were some. Let's see…" Mr. Reynolds looked off into space. "Some say Captain Kidd buried treasure at the Shoals. Of course, some will argue that Captain Kidd was never really a pirate, but was set up for political reasons to appear to be one. You see…"

Will stopped Mr. Reynolds in mid-sentence. "When? When was he here?"

"Well, I'm not sure exactly, but he was hanged in 1701."

Rachel and Will gave knowing glances to each other. Clearly, the treasure could not have belonged to Captain Kidd.

One of the coins was dated 1708. That was seven years *after* Captain Kidd had been hanged.

Mr. Reynolds continued. "There was John Quelch. He supposedly buried a hundred-thousand dollars on the Isles. He was hung, too, in Boston in 1704."

Rachel and Will eyed each other again. It couldn't have been Quelch's coins.

Rachel leaned forward in her seat. "When was Blackbeard here?"

Mr. Reynolds didn't miss a beat. "Later than the other two."

Will jumped in. "But when? Would he have been here after 1708?"

This time Rachel did try to kick Will under the table. She was only able to give a glancing blow to the cuff of his jeans.

He smirked at her when she missed him.

Rachel was sure Mr. Reynolds would start asking them questions now. Why would anyone just casually ask about 1708?

"Will! Didn't I tell you I wanted ranch dressing?" His father's voice was sharp and harsh.

Will tensed. "Not until after I poured Italian all over the salad."

Rachel's fork was twisted full of spaghetti, but she was afraid to try to place it into her mouth. She might have to say something to help. Will used to let his father's remarks roll off his back. Recently he had trouble doing that.

"Next time, ask first," Mr. Reynolds directed.

Will picked up his fork and stabbed another piece of tomato as he spoke. "Italian dressing was a good choice. This is an Italian meal."

Mr. Reynolds gave Will a sideways look and Rachel made her move. "Uh, Mr. Reynolds…uh…who else was here? Who was here in, let's say…1708? What about Blackbeard?" Now she was babbling.

Mr. Reynolds looked away from Will and straight at her. He smiled awkwardly and spoke using his teacher voice. "Well, let's see. You've asked a lot of questions all at once."

Rachel felt heat in her face and knew her skin was turning red. Fortunately, Mr. Reynolds went into lecture mode. "Well, Blackbeard was certainly the best known of the pirates in this area. I believe there was another pirate here about the same time. He was called 'The Scot', but I don't know too much about him." He again rolled his spaghetti onto his fork perfectly. Not a single strand dangled. "Blackbeard spent time here and in the Carolinas. He died around 1718."

Will beamed at Rachel. She nodded back. It all fit. The coins could definitely have belonged to Blackbeard. Or to some pirate named The Scot.

Mr. Reynolds watched their exchanges. "Why the sudden

interest in local pirates?"

Rachel swallowed hard.

Will answered. "No reason. Just interested."

Mr. Reynolds looked skeptical.

Will continued, "I told Rachel that Blackbeard used to come to this area, and she didn't believe me."

Rachel shot Will a glare. That's just what she wanted. Mr. Reynolds would now think she was stupid.

Will just shrugged at her when his father wasn't looking.

Mr. Reynolds gave her a displeased look. "Rachel, you should have studied this when you were in fourth grade. Who was your teacher? Wasn't it Ms. Monet?"

Oh boy, Rachel thought. Now she was going to get Ms. Monet in trouble just because she hadn't paid attention during the lessons on pirates. "I think I was sick or something when we had pirates."

Will snorted as he tried to stifle a laugh.

"Dad, didn't Blackbeard bury treasure out at the Shoals and never go back for it?"

Mr. Reynolds nodded.

Rachel asked, "Why would he do that? I mean, why would he leave it there?"

Mr. Reynolds reached for some bread. "I don't think he meant to leave it." He split the bread with his fingers. "I'm sure he had every intention of returning for it. He left his wife there to protect the treasure for him. Supposedly, she waited for years for him to return before she died. Some even say she still haunts the island."

Rachel felt a tingle again.

Will asked, "Do you know which one of the islands?"

Mr. Reynolds thought for a moment. "I'm pretty certain it was Smuttynose." He hesitated, "Or was it Lunging?" He cleared his throat uncomfortably. Mr. Reynolds was rarely unsure of anything, and Rachel figured not knowing was freaking him out. "Anyway, supposedly she haunts one of them."

Will grinned. "Rachel's afraid of ghosts."

Rachel knew her face was even redder now. She swung her foot at Will. This time she connected.

****

"Rachel, would you like some ice cream for dessert?" Mr. Reynolds asked when they'd finished their meal.

"No thank you," she answered. "I should go home, but the dinner was really good. May I help you clean up?"

"No," Will's father actually smiled. "No, you go ahead. I'm glad you enjoyed it. I'm afraid I'm not the cook that Mrs. Reynolds is."

Will rolled his eyes and said sharply, "You never told her that." Mr. Reynolds shot a hard look in Will's direction and Will quickly mumbled, "Sorry." Will nudged Rachel's arm. "Before you go, let's go up to my room. I have a book I want to show you."

Mr. Reynolds said, "Yes you have that volume on pirates your mother and I gave you for your birthday. Don't forget to call her."

"It's not even 8:00 yet."

"I know, I'm just reminding you," Mr. Reynolds answered.

"Do you want to talk to her when I'm done?" Will asked hopefully.

"If she wishes to speak with me, I'll speak with her."

Will looked as if he was about to say something else to his father, but quickly turned and said to Rachel, "C'mon. The book's in my room."

They bounded up the stairs two at a time and went into Will's bedroom. The bedroom windows faced the backyard. The woods were so dense beyond the yard that he rarely closed the window blinds.

The room was a mass of clutter. It wasn't dirty, but it was hard to find a spot of carpet that wasn't covered by clothes, magazines or sports equipment.

Will walked over to the small bookcase and ran his finger

along the book spines. "Here it is!"

He sat down on the floor with his back supported by his bed. Rachel sat down next to him. Will flipped through until he found the section on Blackbeard. "Listen to this, 'Edward Teach or Thatch, also known as Blackbeard, was one of the most notorious pirates who ever sailed.'"

"That was his real name? Edward Teach or Edward Thatch?" Rachel asked.

"I guess," Will answered and continued reading aloud, "'Little is known about his early life, but most believe he lived in England prior to becoming a pirate. It is not clear when he turned to piracy, however, he began gaining attention in 1716.'"

Rachel stopped him. "Will, the coins are from much earlier than that."

"Yeah, but as long as they aren't dated after he died, they could still belong to him."

Rachel thought about Will's response for a moment and then stood up and reached into her front pocket. She pulled out two quarters, two dimes, a nickel and two pennies.

Will watched. "What are you doing?"

"Checking the dates on the coins in my pocket." She held up each coin and read the dates. "The quarters are dated 2002 and 1974! Geez! I didn't know I was carrying around such an old coin." She nodded to Will. "I guess you're right.

Blackbeard could have had coins from any date before the time he died."

Rachel read off the dates of the other coins. "The dimes are 1996 and 1990, the nickel is 1999, and the pennies are from 1995 and 1976." She looked at Will. "What do you have?"

Will rolled on his side and reached into his pocket. "I have two quarters and a penny. The penny is from 1966! The quarters look new. They're from 2002 and 2001."

"Okay," Rachel concluded as she pocketed her cash and sat back down. "I'm convinced. If I can have a coin dated 1974 and you have one from 1966, the coins could be Blackbeard's."

Will left his coins on the floor and continued. "'Teach first served under the command of Benjamin Hornigold. In 1716, Hornigold gave Teach a captured vessel and a small crew. In 1717, they captured a French ship.'"

"Hey," Rachel interrupted. "That explains how he could have had a franc!"

Will grinned. "I was thinking the same thing. More proof that the coins belonged to Blackbeard." He continued. "'Hornigold was granted amnesty...'"

"What's that?"

"I think it means they forgave him for being a pirate," Will explained, "'but Blackbeard continued with piracy.'"

"Does it say anything about the Isles of Shoals?" Rachel

tried to hurry him along. "I can't stay too much longer."

Will scanned through a couple of pages. "Wow, listen to this! It says, 'according to legend, one night Blackbeard sat in his cabin with a couple of members of his crew. As they were drinking, Blackbeard suddenly drew out two pistols and then put his hands under the table.'" Will looked over at Rachel with a glint in his eyes. "'Blackbeard cocked the guns. One of the crew members ran out of the cabin, but the other stayed. Blackbeard blew out the candle on the table and fired one of the guns. The crew member was hit in the knee leaving him permanently lame!'"

Rachel's eyes were wide. "Whoa!"

"Wow!" Will exclaimed. "See. I told you he was a real blood-thirsty pirate!"

Rachel simply shook her head in amazement. "Does it say anything about the Isles of Shoals?"

Will was still grinning. "Okay, okay." He continued scanning the pages.

"And what about The Scot? Your dad mentioned a guy named The Scot?" Rachel added.

Will kept flipping through pages. "No, I don't see anything about a pirate named The Scot."

"Is there an index in the back?"

"No, wait. Here's something on the Isles of Shoals." Will

read aloud, "'Blackbeard is believed to have spent time at the Isles of Shoals, a group of islands located off the coasts of Maine and New Hampshire. In particular, it is thought that he lived on Smuttynose Island where legend has it that he buried treasure. After a trip to England, Blackbeard returned to the Isles of Shoals with a young woman. Blackbeard instructed the woman to guard his treasure until he returned. He then sailed away, never to return. She died many years later and according to legend her ghost remains on the island protecting his treasure.'" He closed the book, holding his place with his finger, and leaned over toward Rachel and whispered, "I'm so scared!"

"Will, don't be a jerk! You never know, maybe she protects the treasure to this day."

"Yeah, right!" Will laughed. "But, there's more. He opened the book again and read, "'Samuel Haley discovered four bars of silver and used the money to build a breakwater connecting Smuttynose to another island. Most believe the silver belonged to Blackbeard.'"

Will said to Rachel, "The ghost didn't protect the treasure if Samuel Haley found it and used it. So we've got nothing to worry about."

Rachel wasn't so sure. "I don't know," she said. "That Haley guy used the silver to build something on the island. So, maybe she did protect it."

"Sure!" Will chuckled for a moment, then stopped. A funny look crossed his face.

A knock on the doorjamb startled both of them. Will's father stood in the doorway. His smile was gone and so was the decent mood. "Will, you need to call your mother."

Rachel jumped up and headed for the door. "I'd better go."

Will jumped up too. "I'll walk you home."

"No, call your mother," Mr. Reynolds instructed.

Will stepped between Rachel and the door. "No, wait. This will just take a couple of minutes and I'll walk with you."

"I…" Rachel looked from Will to Mr. Reynolds.

"She's scared to walk by herself," Will told his father. He grabbed Rachel's hand and headed down the stairs for the den, dragging her along with him. "This won't take long. She may not even be home," Will told her.

Rachel punched him in the arm as they entered the den. "You dope! Why did you have to say I was scared?"

Will shrugged. "I don't know. I wanted to walk you home. It just came out."

Rachel rolled her eyes, but understood. Sometimes things popped out of her mouth, too. She flopped down onto a chair while Will dialed the number. She didn't want to touch any-thing. This was Mr. Reynolds' den and he was very particular about people moving things around. She remembered him yelling at them for putting his dictionary back on the wrong shelf of the bookcase.

"I don't think she's home." Will pulled the phone away from his mouth as he talked to Rachel. "I'll just leave a message and…oh, hi Mom. It's me."

Rachel sat and listened to Will's side of the conversation. It was pretty boring, consisting of a lot of yeahs and okays. There was nothing interesting until it appeared the conversation was coming to an end. It was then that Will said the words Rachel dreaded, "Okay Mom. I'll work out a time with Dad to come out to see you."

Rachel sat straight up in the chair and stared at Will. He looked over at her with that pathetic 'what can I do?' look and shrugged his shoulders.

"Mom, don't cry. I'll be out soon."

Chapter Six

Rachel's stomach felt like it had dropped to the floor. She immediately stood up and headed for the door. Will reached out to stop her but missed her arm. He pulled the phone off the desk. It clattered loudly on the hardwood floor.

Rachel didn't stop. She didn't even look back.

From the other room Will's father shouted, "Will! What's all the racket?"

Rachel reached the front door, clumsily unlocked it, and slammed it on the way out. She ran across the lawn and headed down the tree-lined street.

She knew this was going to happen and Mr. Reynolds' behavior had just insured that Will would want to go to see his mother. In fact, it was likely Will would want to go and live with his mother. Rachel wouldn't want to live with Will's father either. He didn't even try to be nice to Will. Tears welled up in her eyes as she ran.

It was getting dark, but the street lamps had not yet come on. Rachel knew she should go home, but didn't want to. She knew if she did there would be questions. Her mother always had questions whenever she came home. Rachel didn't want to answer any questions. She didn't want to answer questions about what had happened during the day. She didn't want to answer questions about Will, and she definitely didn't want to answer questions about why she was crying.

The air had cooled since the sun had gone down, but it was still warm. There was a slight breeze that carried the saltwater scent of the ocean. Rachel continued down the darkening street toward the water.

Rachel was focused on her own thoughts. She had always expected Will to be there when she wanted him. They didn't always get along. In fact, they argued a lot, but they always saw the other's side. Not this time. Will would not be around for her. And, what about their business? What about all the plans they had made to hang out at the beach?

Rachel spun around suddenly. Something had broken her train of thought. She looked back down the street that she had just walked. It was now almost completely dark. She scanned both sides of the street quickly, but saw nothing. All Rachel could hear was the dull roar of the surf.

She was just about convinced her mind was playing tricks on her when out of the corner of her eye she saw a small movement in the darkness on her side of the street. It was near a house half a block away. Perhaps the movement came from the bushes surrounding the front porch. Then she saw it move once again.

Rachel tensed. She turned immediately toward the beach and quickened her pace. She knew she had made a mistake. Even though Olde Locke Beach was a safe area, she knew she shouldn't be out walking around in the dark alone. Rachel could try to head home, but she would have to go back the way she came. And that was where someone or something waited. Her eyes searched the darkness. Why weren't the street lamps on?

Rachel took several more steps in the direction of the lights coming from the boardwalk at the beach. Suddenly, from behind her, she heard the sound of pounding feet moving quickly in her direction. She didn't turn around. That would waste precious time. Rachel took off in a full run toward the boardwalk. She would be safe if she could get there.

The pounding of the feet behind her were now drowned out by the pounding of her own feet. She felt her breath getting short even though she had only run the length of a block. A feeling of panic was starting to sweep over her.

How could she have been so careless? Rachel was always aware of her surroundings—except when she let her mind wander, which is exactly what had happened. She had been too busy worrying about Will's trip to California to pay attention to where she was.

Rachel kept running full speed toward the beach. Her breathing was becoming more difficult and she worried that she wouldn't be able to keep up the pace all the way to the boardwalk.

Her mind raced. Should she scream? Should she call for help? But, given that she was out of breath, she was afraid very little would come out. Maybe she should try to go to one of the houses and bang on the door. Maybe...

Then, from behind her, she heard, "Rach! Hey Rachel!"

Rachel knew that voice. That voice belonged to Will. Thank goodness. Rachel slowed down the pace and looked behind her. But when she looked back, Will wasn't there.

"Rachel!" She heard him again. Then she saw him. He was on the opposite side of the street still running toward her. Had he been behind her the whole time? She knew the answer was no. Rachel scanned the darkness behind her. The footsteps had been much closer. And the pounding feet had been on the same side of the street. She watched Will run toward her, but even now, she didn't hear his steps.

Will crossed the street and caught up with her. He was out of breath, too. "Didn't you hear me call you? I've been yelling."

Rachel shook her head. No, she hadn't heard him. Well, that is until she finally heard him and turned around. But before, all she had heard were pounding feet right behind her.

"Rachel!" Will insisted, "Why didn't you answer me?"

"Were you on my side of the street?" she asked him.

"What? What are you talking about?"

Rachel looked back down the street. "Were you on my side of the street?" she repeated the question.

Will gave her a blank look as he shook his head. "No, you saw me. I was on the other side."

"Did you cross over there after coming up behind me?"

He shook his head, again. Rachel believed him. She knew Will wouldn't lie about this. Besides, she knew it wasn't possible.

"Somebody was behind me," she told him.

"Yeah, me!"

"No Will, someone was behind me, on this side of the street—chasing me. I know it."

"Oh geez." Will said and rolled his eyes. "Yeah, it must have been a ghost." He tried to make an eerie noise, but it came out sounding more like the moan he let out the last time he had a stomachache.

"Shut up!" She pushed him. "I'm serious."

"Rachel, you have ghosts on the brain. You probably just imagined it."

Now Rachel was angry. She hadn't imagined it.

Or had she? Her eyes tracked back down the street. She certainly didn't see anyone now. Maybe the person ducked out of sight when she turned around or when Will started down the street.

Will was staring at her now.

Rachel shouted at him. "I know what I saw!" She defended herself, but secretly wondered if maybe he was right. Maybe it was all in her head. Maybe the talk of ghosts was getting to her.

"Okay!" Will said. "Whatever! But you left so fast we didn't get to finish talking."

Rachel relaxed a bit. Will could be pretty sweet sometimes. He had followed her to sort things out, to reassure her that everything would be okay. "You go first," she said.

"You left so fast we didn't get a chance to divide up the coins."

"Oh Will! You're such a jerk!" Rachel turned in a huff and started for home. Will followed, but at a distance.

Chapter Seven

Rachel pushed cereal around in a bowl with her spoon. She had only eaten half of it, but it was already soggy. She couldn't shake the eerie feeling that someone had followed her the night before and that it had not been Will. Rachel fished the raisins out with her spoon and ate those. Raisins didn't get soggy.

"Hey," Steve said as he came into the kitchen. He grabbed a bowl from the cupboard and joined her at the small kitchen table.

Rachel asked, "What are you doing home?"

"Dentist appointment." Steve picked up the cereal box that set on the table and poured some into a bowl.

Rachel's older brother, Steve, was usually long gone by the time Rachel got up. Lobstermen never sleep late.

"What's your problem?" Steve asked with a mouthful of

cereal and milk. "You look like you lost your best friend."

"I might," Rachel responded glumly. When Steve looked puzzled, she continued, "Will's going to visit his mom in California."

"Tough break."

Rachel nodded. That was the only part of her worries she was willing to share with Steve. "You and Dad go out to the Shoals, right?"

Steve nodded and chewed. "Sometimes, but we put the lobster traps in closer to the shore off the mainland." He stopped chewing his cereal and looked at her suspiciously. "But, you know that already."

It was true. She did know that.

"Why the sudden interest in the Shoals?"

"I was just asking."

"You've never been especially interested in the history around here before." He eyed her closely.

"I know. I thought it might be fun to go out there for a picnic or something. Maybe before Will leaves."

Steve was still suspicious, but he seemed to buy her explanation. "Most of the islands are privately owned and you can't go out on them." Steve talked with a mouthful of cereal. "You can take the ferry to Star Island."

"What about Smuttynose?" Rachel asked him.

"Yeah, I went out there once with a small group from the high school. There's a walking trail."

"Anything interesting ever happen on Smuttynose?" She tried not to be as obvious as Will had been.

"The Spanish ship Sagunto was ripped apart on the rocks in the 1800's. Some of the men got to shore, but died before they could get to a house for help."

Rachel could feel her skin tingle. "Why did they die if they made it to shore?"

Steve looked over his heaping spoonful of cereal and said, "Because it happened at night during a storm in January."

"Oh." Rachel ate another raisin. Well, there was nothing ghostly about that. The weather at that time would have been freezing.

Steve continued, "And a couple of women were murdered out there."

Oh great, Rachel thought. "Have you heard stories about ghosts out there?"

"Oh sure."

Rachel tensed and asked, "But, none of these ghosts have been spotted on the mainland, right? I mean, they stay out on the Shoals, right?"

Steve finished the last bit of cereal. "As far as I know." He looked at her with a sparkle in his eyes, "But there's always a first time!"

"Dope!"

Steve laughed as he got up from the table. After rinsing the bowl and spoon and placing them in the dishwasher, he left.

Rachel knew she was being silly. Ghosts. How ridiculous. It couldn't have been a ghost following her the previous night. A ghost wouldn't have to follow anyone. A ghost could just take whatever she wanted. Couldn't she? In fact, probably no one was following her. Will was right. She was just letting her imagination run away with her.

Rachel's mother came through the garage entrance carrying two shopping bags. "Did Steve leave for his dental appointment?" she asked as she set the bags on the counter. Before Rachel could answer, she added, "I got hung up at the grocery store and was worried Steve would sleep through the appointment."

Rachel began to unload one bag while her mother unpacked the other. "He had cereal with me and then left a few minutes ago."

Mrs. Clark stopped unpacking and looked at Rachel. "Did he brush his teeth after he ate?"

"I don't think so." Rachel shrugged.

"Oh dear," Mrs. Clark muttered.

"What's the big deal?" Rachel asked. "The dentist is going

to clean his teeth anyway. Now you'll get your money's worth."

"Oh Rachel." Mrs. Clark frowned as she removed lettuce, tomatoes and carrots from one of the bags.

"Mom, do you believe in ghosts?" Rachel asked as she opened the pantry and started to put away the sugar and flour.

"Of course dear."

"What?" Rachel pulled her head out of the pantry. She couldn't possibly have heard her mother correctly. "Mom, for a second, I thought you said yes."

Mrs. Clark smiled at her. "I did say yes, dear. I do believe there are ghosts. There are lots of stories of ghost sightings in New England."

Rachel shivered. "Have you ever seen one? A ghost, I mean."

"Well, no," Mrs. Clark conceded. "But there are so many stories that I think it must be true. Besides, I believe you saw one."

Rachel had seen a ghost. Well, she was ninety-nine percent sure she had. Rachel's mother had always said she believed Rachel. But, sometimes she wondered whether her mother was just trying to make her feel better. Until recently, Rachel hadn't thought of the incident for a long time. She had only been seven at the time it happened.

Rachel put a package of dry spaghetti on the shelf and asked, "Do you believe any of the stories from around here, like at the Isles of Shoals?"

"Chicken?" her mother asked.

Rachel cringed. "Geez Mom! Maybe a little, but it's because I saw a ghost when I was only seven!"

"Rachel," Mrs. Clark smiled gently as she held up a package of chicken from the grocery store. "I meant for dinner."

"Oh," Rachel's face reddened. "Yeah, sure, whatever," she mumbled.

Maybe she was jumping to conclusions. Rachel stuck her face deeper into the pantry so her mother couldn't see her.

Mrs. Clark put the package into the refrigerator and said, "The image you saw that night frightened you, but never tried to hurt you."

What her mother said was true. She never felt she was in danger. Actually, she wasn't even frightened at the time. It was later, after she thought about it, that the experience unnerved her.

Mrs. Clark said, "It might help to talk about it."

A sudden knock on the side door saved her. She didn't want to talk about it. Rachel immediately went to see who it was. It was Will.

"We need to get out to the Shoals," he blurted out before Rachel could stop him.

Mrs. Clark popped her head around the door. "Oh, hi Will. Do you want some breakfast?"

Rachel noticed that her mom had been making a special effort to talk to Will since his mother had moved to California. Rachel usually appreciated this, but not right now. "No Mom," she answered for Will.

"Rachel, I think Will is capable of answering for himself. Besides, I've never known him to turn down food." Mrs. Clark smiled at him.

"No thanks," Will responded. "I had some leftover spaghetti from last night."

"Oh." That left her mother with nothing more to say.

Rachel seized the opportunity and slipped out the door, closing it quickly behind her. "Geez, Will!"

"Well, how should I know your mom was hiding behind the door?" Will said while unfolding a piece of paper. He shoved the paper in front of her. It was a ferry schedule.

Will spoke, "I looked this up on the web last night. We can catch the 9:25 ferry to Star Island at the Isles of Shoals. It costs fifteen dollars apiece and I have the cash."

"What! Fifteen dollars apiece! Are you feeling okay?" Will never wanted to spend money foolishly, or for any reason for that matter. It was save, save, save.

"I figure it's worth it if we find more treasure!" he told her.

"Come on! We don't have a lot of time. The bus picks up on Ocean Road at 9:00. It will get us to the dock by 9:20. That will give us five minutes to buy our tickets and get on board."

Rachel looked at her watch. It was 8:45. "But, I'm supposed to..."

"The ferry will be back by 1:00." He looked at her pleadingly. "Please, please, please!"

"How do we know..."

"Please, please, please! I have the money!"

"Oh," Rachel gave an exasperated sigh. "Okay." Rachel opened the door and shouted inside. "I'm going with Will." She didn't wait for a response, but grabbed a sweatshirt on the hook by the door and closed the door behind her.

"Where are the coins?" Will asked her once they had taken a few steps away from the house.

Rachel patted the right front pocket of her shorts.

Chapter Eight

The bus dropped Rachel and Will off right across the street from the ferry landing. Cars zipped into the lot as last minute hopefuls tried to book passage. Rachel and Will dashed across the street as soon as the light turned green. Fortunately, only one man was in line to get tickets.

"Can we get on by ourselves?" Rachel whispered to Will as they got in line behind the man. At twelve they were able to ride most types of public transportation without an adult, but she had never tried to ride the ferry.

Will looked alarmed. "I don't know." Then suddenly he said in a very loud voice, "Okay!" and waved toward the ferry. "We'll be right there!"

Will was so convincing, Rachel looked up at the ferry half expecting to see someone she knew. But, of course, she didn't. It was just a ploy to avoid having the ticket agent ask any questions.

The man in front of them finished his transaction and they were next. Rachel hoped the agent had been paying attention to Will's outburst.

Will spoke rapidly. "Two please. We're both twelve and my mom will be really upset if we miss this ferry." Before the ticket agent could respond, Will stepped out of line and waved to the ferry again. "We're coming!"

Rachel bit her lip to keep from laughing. This was not like Will at all. First he was willing to spend money and now this display of acting—or was it fibbing? Rachel looked up at the agent and forced an innocent smile. "I'm with him and we're both twelve," she managed to say.

"Thirty dollars, please."

Will thrust the money into the ticket agent's hand and grabbed the two tickets she extended toward them. He turned to Rachel and said, "We've got to hurry!"

They handed their tickets to a young girl at the entrance of the dock and ran up the gangplank. Rachel and Will worked their way through the throng of people gathered by the gangplank and sat down on a bench at the rail. "I can't believe you did that!" she said to him. "Usually you turn red and talk too much when you lie."

"Who lied?" he asked. "All I said to the passengers was that we'd be right there. And," he grinned at her, "I told the agent we are both twelve, which is true."

Rachel bought the story only to a point. "What about when you told the ticket agent your mom would be upset if we missed the ferry?"

Will did not miss a beat. "That was true. She would be upset. This trip could end up making us rich!"

Rachel smiled. She was the one who usually came up with rationalizations, and usually Will gave her a bad time about it. Maybe he was loosening up, she thought. Rachel took a deep breath and relaxed. Maybe this day trip out to the Isles of Shoals would answer some of their questions. Rachel turned to look at the other passengers. Her feelings of relief were short-lived. Staring directly at them were the two teenage boys from the beach. Not far from them was the fair man in khaki pants.

Rachel grabbed Will's wrist. When he looked over at her, she nodded toward the boys. Rachel felt Will's arm stiffen when he saw the teens. She nodded again and Will looked toward the man.

"Who's he?" Will asked.

"He was watching us on the beach right before I found the coins."

Just then, the Captain announced that passengers should

cover their ears. Both Rachel and Will cupped their hands tightly over their ears, and the Captain sounded the horn. It was loud and drawn out. Will started to laugh and nudged Rachel with his elbow. She followed his gaze and laughed too. A woman was walking while holding two cups of coffee. She cringed as the horn's blast continued, but couldn't cover her ears and carry the cups at the same time.

Rachel suddenly stopped laughing. The woman with the coffee was the lady on the beach with the big hat who had played a game of "keep away" with Greta. Rachel watched as she handed one of the cups of coffee to the man in the khaki pants. Khaki Man and Hat Lady were together.

The ferry began to pull away from the dock. Immediately the wind whipped up and Rachel put on the sweatshirt she had been holding. Her long brown hair blew straight out from her head and smacked Will in the face. He sputtered, and brushed it away with his hand.

Rachel stood up casually and walked to the far end of the ferry out of sight of the boys and the couple. She signaled Will and he followed her. They leaned against the rail and looked out over the Atlantic Ocean and coastline as the ferry made its way to the Isles of Shoals. Water splashed up from the sea spraying both their faces.

"That lady is the one from the beach. Do you think they

followed us?" Rachel asked as the ferry crashed through the whitecaps.

"No," Will answered as he looked back over his shoulder at their traveling companions. "Well, I don't think so."

The triple-deck ferry moved quickly through the water. They sped past the red brick buildings that lined the wharf. A white church steeple spiraled above the brick structures up into the deep blue sky. Four red tugboats bounced in the swell waiting for work.

Rachel turned to Will and spoke. "Let's stay away from those boys."

Will bristled. "I can handle them! They just caught me off guard at the beach."

"Will, we don't want them getting in our way when we get to Star Island. We're going to have to try to avoid them."

"Yeah, okay. But, I can handle them."

"I'd help," she volunteered, "but only in an emergency." She smiled at him.

Will smiled back, so she bit her tongue and didn't finish her thought. She didn't point out that the teens were both several inches taller and several pounds heavier than Will. It wasn't likely he could handle them alone. "Let's go up to the top deck," Rachel suggested.

They climbed the flight of stairs, holding tightly to the rail.

The ferry pitched and tilted as it cut through the whitecaps. The closer to the top deck they got, the windier it became. Once again, Rachel's hair flew straight back right into Will's face.

Sputtering, Will asked, "Do you have something to tie back your hair?"

Rachel reached back and held her hair away from him. "No." She stuffed her hair inside her collar.

"Look over there," Will said. "It's that guy from the Isles View Hotel." Standing at the top rail was a tall man with short dark hair. Rachel didn't remember him, but Will had spent more time at the hotel.

"That's unbelievable. At least five people from the hotel are on the same ferry," Will said. "It's like this is the only ferry in town!"

Rachel placed her hand on Will's shoulder and looked him in the eye. "Will, I hate to break it to you, but this *is* the only ferry in town."

"Oh," he stifled an embarrassed chuckle. "Well, it's still weird." Then he crossed his eyes at her.

Rachel smiled, but had to agree. It was strange. Even though it was the only ferry, why was it such a popular place?

A voice boomed over the outside loudspeaker pointing out the landmarks. They passed a lighthouse, a fort, and a prison. Rachel had seen these landmarks several times while out on her father's lobster boat, but had never really paid any attention to them.

She looked out toward the sea and noticed the whitecaps. "How long does this trip take?" Rachel asked. "It's pretty rough today."

"I think I heard someone say forty-five minutes to an hour." Will looked down at the water, but lifted his head quickly and turned to face the inside of the boat.

"What's the matter?" Rachel studied him.

"Nothing," he said.

Rachel rolled her eyes. "You can't be sick already. We've hardly left the pier!"

"Yeah, well you tell my stomach that!"

Rachel shook her head in disbelief. "Well, don't look down at the water. Look out toward the horizon."

Will nodded.

"Do you think it would help if you ate something?" she asked. "There's a snack bar with sandwiches and drinks."

Will shook his head. "I think I should stay out here and breathe the fresh air."

"Okay, I'm going down to get some hot chocolate," she told him.

Will walked to the long bench at the rail. Rachel watched him lie down. She started toward the stairs to the lower level, but first scanned the deck area. She didn't see Khaki Man, Hat Lady or the two teenage boys. Rachel glanced back at Will. She hesitated about leaving him alone on the bench, but saw an elderly couple across from him. Besides, the pilothouse was on this deck and the announcer was there. Will would be fine.

Rachel went down two flights of stairs and entered the eating area from the bottom deck. It was two stories with a staircase in the middle. Both levels were enclosed and had several tables for passengers. A number of people were seated inside eating sandwiches and drinking warm drinks. Others were simply sitting at the tables looking out of the windows, probably to get out of the wind.

Rachel saw Khaki Man and Hat Lady sitting at one of the tables by the windows. Rachel ordered her hot chocolate and exited the eating area from the second deck after climbing the center staircase. Rachel took a seat next to Will. She looked at her watch as the ferry bounced closer to the Isles of Shoals. Will was sound asleep.

Rachel settled back and sipped her hot chocolate.

****

The Isles of Shoals were in clear view now. They looked more like very large boulders than islands. There were no trees and a small amount of grass and other plants seemed to take shelter near a few weathered buildings scattered about. Rachel heard a woman comment to a companion. "Pretty rustic looking."

As the ferry entered the harbor, Rachel shook Will's shoulders until he woke up. It took a bit of effort on her part. Will was dead to the world. "Will, wake up! We're here!"

Will staggered to his feet. They stood on the top deck and looked out over Star Island. A large, white structure with an open porch stood starkly in the foreground. They could also see the neighboring island of Smuttynose. "Look at how rocky the islands are," Rachel observed. "How could you hide treasure here?"

Will held a hand up, shading his eyes from the glare of the sun reflecting off of the water. "I was thinking the same thing."

"Geez, the whole world could see someone trying to hide something."

Will nodded.

Rachel pointed to the end of Smuttynose that was closest to Star Island. "I'm not sure we can get over there," Rachel said. "It looks like the islands are connected by a breakwater, but we may not be able to cross it. In fact, it looks like there is an island in between. Are there two breakwaters?"

"Rachel, we have to get out there!"

Rachel was not convinced they would.

As the ferry reached the dock, there were several people waiting. They started chanting in unison. "You Will Come Back! You Will Come Back!" Others shouted, "You Did Come Back! You Did Come Back!"

Within moments the ferry was docked at the pier and Rachel and Will made their way down the gangplank. "What was that about?" Will said to Rachel.

Rachel shrugged. "And, what's with the suitcases?" Rachel watched several people struggle with luggage and bags as they crossed the pier. A man moving quickly by them carrying a suitcase said, "The hotel is used as a conference center during the summer months. Some of these passengers won't take the ferry back until next week."

"How about you?" Rachel inquired.

"I'm staying," he said and then disappeared into the crowd.

Will spun around in a circle as they walked up the pier. "Those guys and the couple are getting off now," he said as he stopped turning and continued to walk toward the flagpole located directly in front of them.

Rachel now turned to check out the teenagers and Khaki Man and Hat Lady. The couple was following along with the group that was headed toward the hotel. The teenaged boys crossed the lawn in front of the hotel and walked over toward the breakwater connecting Star and Smuttynose.

"Hey," Will said as he spotted the teens. "They're going to Smuttynose!" Will turned to follow them.

"Will, wait!" Rachel began, but was interrupted.

Chapter Nine

A loud voice boomed behind them. "Everyone who wants to go on the island tour needs to meet at the flagpole."

"We've got to be nonchalant," Rachel whispered.

"What?"

"You know," she explained. "We can't draw any attention to ourselves."

"Yeah, okay, but we don't have much time to get over to Smuttynose," Will said. "And, I'm not going to let those guys beat us to any treasure."

Most of the day-trip passengers moved toward the flagpole for the tour. Those with suitcases and backpacks climbed up the stairs to the hotel.

"I'm going to take the tour," Rachel said. "When you fell asleep, the guide said the tour would include history of the

Isles of Shoals and the early people who lived here." Rachel's eyes gleamed. "Including the pirates who lived here."

"Good idea." Will looked out toward Smuttynose. "I'm going to find out if we can get over to Smuttynose from here."

He turned to walk away and Rachel grabbed his arm. "Don't get into a fight with those boys, and don't go over to Smuttynose without me."

"Okay." She didn't let go of his arm. "I promise," he told her, and then she let go.

Rachel watched Will cross the expansive lawn at the front of the hotel as the tour guide arrived at the flagpole.

"I'm Joe. We're on Star Island and this is the former Oceanic Hotel." The tour guide began speaking. "The building that you now see in front of you was opened in 1876. It is a combination of preexisting structures." Rachel stopped listening. It opened too late for it to have any importance to them.

Instead, she stepped out of the crowd and looked for Will. She could not see him or the teenaged boys. For a moment, she thought about going after Will, but changed her mind when Joe started moving the tour group away from the flagpole.

Rachel and the group followed the guide around the right side of the hotel. Laundry was hanging in plain view and water was being pumped from the ferry to the hotel.

"If you look out across the water, you can see White and

Lunging Islands. Notice the automated lighthouse on White," Joe explained.

"What's that building on Lunging?" someone called out.

"That's a private residence," Joe answered, then continued with his narration, "it's believed that a double wedding took place out on the islands in 1716 or 1717. The notorious pirates known as Blackbeard and The Scot married their brides and lived out there for a period of time."

Rachel perked up. The Scot! Finally they might get some information about him.

Joe paused and smiled. "Of course, it's not quite as romantic as it sounds. The poor young woman who married Blackbeard was wife number thirteen or fourteen. Then he sailed away and left her to guard his treasure, but never returned. Some say she still haunts the islands waiting for him. Dressed in white, with long blond hair, she wanders the banks saying, 'He will come back. He will come back!'"

Rachel shivered.

"Hey, that's what they say when the ferry docks!" a young boy stated.

"Exactly! They'll say it again when you leave," Joe said and continued, "The Scot lived on White and Blackbeard lived on Lunging."

"What?" Rachel said aloud. A few people turned and

looked at her. She felt her face turning red. "Excuse me," Rachel waved her hand at the guide. "I thought Blackbeard lived over on Smuttynose."

"Well, there are a lot of theories," Joe answered. "Some believe treasure is buried out here on Lunging." He pointed out to the small island. "They've searched extensively, but they didn't find anything, but who knows?"

"Didn't someone discover treasure on Smuttynose that belonged to Blackbeard?" It was a female voice from the back of the group. Rachel stood on her toes to see the speaker, but she couldn't. She wondered if it was Hat Lady.

"Some treasure *was* found out on Smuttynose that was believed to have belonged to Blackbeard or some of his crew members." Joe smiled.

"The story goes that Samuel Haley, who owned Smuttynose, found silver bars near his home in 1820. In fact, you can see the home on Smuttynose today. Haley used the money from the sale of the bars of silver to build a breakwater."

Joe turned and started up a small embankment. Rachel held back for a moment and let the others go by. She gazed out at the two small islands. They weren't far away, but there was no way out to them from Star. Both were very small, much smaller than Star. It was hard to imagine living on those tiny islands, let alone burying treasure there.

"Can people go out to the other islands?" Rachel called out to Joe.

Joe swung around and walked backwards while he answered Rachel's question. "No, the owners of White and Lunging don't allow visitors."

"What about Smuttynose?" she called again.

"Yes, but you need a boat." Joe turned back around and continued walking.

Rachel was deep in thought about Blackbeard, The Scot, and their wives when Will suddenly placed his hand on Rachel's shoulder. She jumped. She turned and shoved him. "Dope! Wear a bell!"

Will laughed. She gave him a warning look and then said, "You just missed everything."

"I heard the last part about needing a boat to get to Smuttynose."

"I guess we can't cross the breakwater then?" Rachel asked.

Will shook his head. "A guy chased me away when I got close. You were right. It looks like there's an island in between Star and Smuttynose. He said there's no way to cross the breakwaters, but..." he hesitated. "I might be able to swim over. It didn't look that far."

Rachel pointed toward Lunging Island. "Don't bother. Joe says Blackbeard's treasure is over there."

"What?"

Rachel quickly told Will about what she had learned.

"Let's go take a look down on the backside of the island," Will suggested. "Maybe we can find something there."

"What about the rest of the tour?"

"I found out what I want to know," Will told her.

Rachel nodded and followed along.

As they walked, they talked, "Did you see those boys?" Rachel asked him.

"They were by the breakwater, but as I got closer, a lady called to them." Will smirked as he said, "I think they're on the island with their mother." He laughed.

Rachel laughed with him. "They definitely won't be a problem!"

"Yeah," Will snickered. "If they give us a hard time, we can tell their *mom*!"

Rachel and Will cut behind the hotel and walked up a slight incline to a large stone structure.

"Hey Will," Rachel said, "this building is a meeting house that was first built in 1685."

"So it would have been here when Blackbeard and The Scot were here."

"Well, sort of," Rachel replied. "It says it was rebuilt in 1720 using wood from a Spanish ship and then it was rebuilt again in 1800, using stone."

Will looked up at the tall steeple.

Rachel continued, "The building has been used as a chapel, a lighthouse, a schoolhouse..."

"A schoolhouse?" Will groaned. "You mean the kids who lived out here that long ago had to go to school?"

Rachel laughed. "It has also been used as a town hall and a courthouse."

Rachel now looked up at the steeple as well. "This is the highest point on the island."

They continued to walk through the grouping of stone buildings. "So this was a town?" Will asked.

"It is the town of Gosport. They told us as we docked—and you slept."

Will and Rachel made their way out of the tiny town center and quickly found themselves on well-worn footpaths surrounded by bushes. They reached a turnstile and continued along a path to a monument. They stopped long enough to see that the monument had been erected in honor of John Smith who first discovered the Isles of Shoals in 1614.

When they started walking again, the paths became less worn and split into many directions. Vegetation and standing water created many dead ends as they tried to reach the edge of the island.

They wandered down several paths only to have to return to the same spot, then chose a path that cut inland, with Rachel leading the way. "Hey Will," she said as she turned to talk to him, but Will was nowhere in sight. Rachel looked back toward the town of Gosport. She could not see any buildings or people. She heard the low-pitch moan of a seagull and felt very much alone. "Will!" she called out again.

Rachel looked back at the path she had just followed. She hadn't noticed that it broke off into other little trails. Now, she was not certain which path she had taken. "Will!"

A seagull swooped down close to her. She ducked down and threw her arms over her head. She could feel the draft caused by the bird's wings. "I'm out of here!" she exclaimed. It came a little too close for comfort.

Rachel called one more time, "Willlllllllllll!"

"Over here!" Will called out to her.

She breathed a sigh of relief as she shouted, "Where are you?"

"Go back down the muddy part of the path until you see the large boulder with water on both sides. Climb over the boulder."

Rachel quickly retraced part of her steps, and followed his instructions. Will met her partway. "Dope!" she said when she found him.

Will grinned at her and said, "Follow me."

Rachel looked around again. Now she could see the steeple and the very top of the hotel roof, but nothing or no one else.

She followed Will along another path and within moments they reached the edge of the island. She had been watching where she stepped because of all the standing water, but suddenly looked up.

"Wow!" she shouted.

Will grinned at her. "It's like you can see forever."

Rachel looked down and planted her feet in a safe spot, then looked out over the Atlantic Ocean. The view was breathtaking. She laughed. "Will, I'll bet we can see England from here."

He laughed, too. "Actually, this was a great spot for pirates. They could easily see an enemy coming."

Rachel nodded in agreement.

"Hey Rach! Come over this way."

Suddenly she had an uneasy feeling. "No, I'm staying here." Rachel sat down on the rocks. The location was beautiful, but very dangerous. One false move on these rocks could be the last. They were also out of view of help. She looked slowly in all directions and saw no one. "Will, maybe we should turn back."

"Rachel," Will's voice sounded exasperated. "You just heard about ghosts again. There isn't anything wrong. It's all in your head."

Rachel's temper flared. "I'm not talking about ghosts!" she retorted. "I'm talking about slipping on the rocks and being out here alone."

Will continued moving away from her. "What's going to happen out here?"

Maybe she was being overly cautious, but she remembered all too well the night before when she had put herself in a bad situation. They shouldn't be out there alone. "Will, I think we should head back."

Will didn't even look back at her. "Why? This is just getting interesting. I'm going to climb over to…"

It was then that she saw that Khaki Man and Hat Lady had followed them. "Will! Turn around!" Rachel stood up.

Will ignored her warning. "Rachel! Go back by yourself."

"Will!"

He stopped, and seeing Rachel's ashen face, finally turned. Rachel saw his body stiffen when he saw Khaki Man and Hat Lady coming into view. He looked at Rachel wide-eyed. Then his eyes searched around. Surrounding them were rocks, large jagged rocks. In front of them was a ledge and the ocean surf below.

Rachel tried to think. *Were* Khaki Man and Hat Lady following them? If so, why? Rachel couldn't imagine a reason that was positive. She looked back at Will. He was too far away from her now. "Come over this way!" she called to Will, but he was already moving in her direction.

Rachel watched as Will shuffled across the rocks as quickly as safety would permit. He slipped once, turning his ankle, but only winced and continued moving. He was worried, too, she thought. And that didn't make her feel any better.

Rachel's heart began to pound faster as she watched the couple coming closer, cornering them. Khaki Man was looking directly at her. It was not a casual look, either, but a deliberate one. He definitely was coming toward them for a reason.

She looked back over at Will. He was closer, almost within reach. She extended her hand toward him as she watched Khaki Man and Hat Lady getting nearer.

Then Rachel saw another person coming up behind them in a full run. It was Joe.

"You can't go over there!" Joe shouted. "Get away from the ledge!"

Will finished his climb over to Rachel as Joe spoke with Khaki Man and Hat Lady. The odd couple gave them one last look then turned to go back to the group as Joe hurried to where Rachel and Will stood.

He panted loudly. "I looked around for you," Joe said to Rachel, "and someone said you had left the tour." He was still out of breath. "At the end of the tour, we tell people not to go out over here."

"Why?" Rachel asked. "It's so beautiful."

Joe nodded his head in agreement. "Gorgeous! But, it's really dangerous out here." Joe pointed to a rock formation close to them and explained, "Years ago, a woman, Miss Underhill, was swept away from that very spot and drowned!"

"Who?"

"She's a lady who came out to the rocks to sit and read while she stayed on the island. Miss Underhill found the area to be beautiful as well and came here each day. But, one day she was swept out to sea and drowned. Ever since, that ledge," he pointed, "has been known as Miss Underhill's Chair."

"Whoa." Rachel said.

She and Will followed Joe back in silence. Rachel felt a lump in her throat as they walked. Although she felt bad about Miss Underhill, she knew there was another reason for how she felt. Had Khaki Man and Hat Lady been following them? "Do you think…?" she started to ask Will.

Will's eyes were wide with uncertainty. "I don't know."

"Let's go back to where there are a lot of people. We'll stay with the group, too, until we get back to the mainland," Rachel said.

"I'm right behind you," Will replied.

Chapter Ten

Rachel walked up the driveway toward her house. She wanted to grab a sandwich and hang out at home for a while. Mainly, she wanted a break from Will. On the ferry ride back from the Isles of Shoals, he had tried to talk her into letting him hold the pouch full of coins. She refused.

Rachel wasn't completely sure why she didn't want to let Will hold onto the coins, or even two of the four. It really wasn't like her not to share with him.

Will accused her of being selfish so she called him a dope. However, she did have to agree with him a little, but she didn't tell him that. Then he started making ghosts noises until she shoved him. They ended up not speaking for the rest of the ferry ride and bus ride home.

As soon as they stepped off the bus, Rachel ducked into

one of the women's clothing shops on the boardwalk. She knew Will wouldn't follow her. She watched through the window as he walked toward the Isles View Hotel. He was going there to do some more work. She knew she should go with him to help, but didn't.

Rachel reached the back door and was just about to enter the house when she saw a note taped to the window pane. She pulled the note off the glass.

There was no envelope, just a piece of white notebook paper folded in half. Rachel unfolded the note and read the words aloud.

"PUT THEM BACK!"

A chill ran up Rachel's spine. The memory of being followed the night before loomed back into her mind. So did thoughts of Khaki Man and Hat Lady. She tried to stop herself from letting her imagination run away with her, but it all poured into her head anyway.

Who could have left the note? "Those teenage boys!" Rachel said aloud. She hadn't liked them since the first time she saw them. Maybe *they* had been following her the night before. Of course, she never saw them so... "Khaki Man and Hat Lady!" she said next. But, they never actually did anything threatening... Suddenly it all came together. "Will!"

****

"We need to talk." Rachel grabbed Will by the arm and swung him around. He spun around so fast he dropped the rake he was holding. "Hey!" he protested loudly.

They stood at the back of the Isles View Hotel.

"Is this your idea of a joke?" Rachel shoved the paper in front of Will's face.

"What are you talking about?" Will took the paper from her hand and examined it. "*My* idea? How should I know where this came from?"

"Because you wrote it!" she accused him. "You probably followed me last night, too." The beach was more crowded today, and a few people turned and looked their way.

"What? Why would I do that?" Will demanded.

"You're trying to scare me, that's why!"

Will repeated the question. "Why would I do that?"

They were standing so close to one another and leaning forward that their noses were almost touching.

"Because you're a jerk!" Rachel fumed, "You want to scare me so that I let you hold on to all of the coins."

"Shhh!" He looked around uncomfortably. "I wouldn't do that!" Will looked hurt for a moment, but then grinned. "It isn't a bad idea though. I wish I'd thought of it."

Rachel clenched her fists and let out a low growl.

"Rachel, I was only kidding you before with the ghost noises. You know I wouldn't really try to scare you, but why won't you let me hold on to the coins?" He looked hurt again.

Rachel gritted her teeth and blurted out, "I'm not letting you hold on to them! Not if you're leaving!" There, she said it. But when the words popped out of her mouth, they even surprised her.

"What?" Will took a step backwards.

Rachel's emotions were all mixed up. She let her knees buckle and sat down on the scraggly lawn. She looked up at Will and said, "This way, you will come back."

Will knelt down next to her. He didn't look mad, just sad. "Rachel, I just want to see my mom."

Some of her anger left. Rachel knew Will missed his mom. "Well, why doesn't she come here to see you?" Rachel argued. "She's the one who moved away. She should be the one who comes out to see you."

Will turned away from her and looked out over the waves.

Rachel kept up the pressure. "You have a life. You shouldn't have to give up your life!"

Will continued to stare across the water as he spoke. "Rachel, she just started a new job. She can't come here for a visit. She just got there!"

Rachel knew that was true, but it wasn't fair. What about his life? What about her life? She got angry again. "I bet you go out there and decide to stay. I bet you won't want to come back." She folded her arms across her chest.

Will now looked over at her and smiled. "That's not going to happen."

"Why? Why won't that happen?"

"Because it won't."

She looked him straight in the eyes. "Well, then, what is going to happen? Have you thought about it?"

"Sure, I've thought about it."

Rachel pushed. "Is your dad going to find a job out there?"

Rachel knew school districts were looking for good teachers just about everywhere. That was one of the reasons Rachel's mom was getting her teaching degree. Even though she and some of the other kids didn't really like Mr. Reynolds as a teacher, she knew he was good. A school district would snap him up in a moment. "Are you going to move permanently?"

Will shook his head and said, "No."

"How do you know?"

"I don't really know what's going on. If I did, I'd tell you."

"Well then, how can you be sure you won't have to move?" Rachel repeated her question. "Have you talked to either of them about it?"

Will just shook his head, no. "I've tried, but neither of them will give me an answer. My dad just changes the subject if I ask what's going to happen, and Mom says things will all work out for the best."

"What does that mean?" Rachel shouted at him.

Will just shrugged. "I don't know."

They sat in silence for what seemed like forever. Then Rachel asked in a low voice, "Do you think they're splitting up?"

Will didn't answer her.

"Will?"

He looked at Rachel and said in a whisper, "I don't know."

There was a deafening roar in Rachel's ears. She wasn't sure if it was the surf or the understanding of what might happen if Will's parents split up. She couldn't even imagine Will not being around. Even though she had existed without him before they met in the second grade, that seemed like a lifetime ago. Rachel's shoulders sagged.

"Now you have to tell me something," he said, clearly wanting to change the subject. "Fair is fair."

Rachel smiled slightly. Changing the subject seemed like a good idea. "Okay."

"Why are you so afraid of ghosts?"

Rachel dug a small hole in the sand. "I'm not afraid. It's

just…"

"It's just what?" he asked.

Rachel turned and said, "If I tell you and you laugh, I'll hit you so hard you'll end up in California without needing a plane!"

Will chuckled. "I'm scared."

Rachel didn't crack a smile. "You should be."

She took a deep breath. "Remember Dr. Anthony?"

Will cocked his head back for a moment. "Yeah. He was a doctor who shared an office with our doctor—Dr. Russo." He paused. "Didn't he pass away a few years ago?"

Rachel nodded her head. "He was my doctor before I started going to Dr. Russo."

Will waited for Rachel to continue.

Rachel took another deep breath. "When I was seven, I woke up one night and Dr. Anthony was standing by my bed looking at me." She stopped, remembering the event. "He didn't say anything, but I felt really calm, like he was just checking on me, so I went back to sleep."

Will watched her, not speaking.

"The next morning, I asked my mom why Dr. Anthony had come over the night before and she got a really funny look on her face." Rachel turned and looked into Will's eyes. "Mom said Dr. Anthony hadn't come to the house, but he had died the night before."

Will's eyes were wide.

Rachel continued. "I always felt he had just come to check on me. You know, like something he still had to do before he left."

"Wow!" Will said. "Are you sure you weren't dreaming the night you saw Dr. Anthony?"

"I wasn't dreaming! Besides, why would I pick that night to dream about him?"

"Okay, okay," he said.

"So, part of me wonders if maybe the ghost of Blackbeard's wife has things she has to do, you know, like protect the coins," Rachel explained. "There have been some weird things going on." She hesitated, "I didn't tell you this before because I thought you'd give me a hard time, but I saw something or someone out at the rocks just before I found the coins. I only caught a glimpse, but I thought it was a woman. I remember seeing yellow and white. When I looked again, she was gone."

"Do you think it could have been a g h o s t?"

Rachel shrugged, but shifted her legs uncomfortably. "I don't know. Maybe. Supposedly, Blackbeard's wife was dressed in white and had long, blond hair."

Will didn't look as though he agreed with her, but he didn't laugh. "I don't think a ghost would leave a note, especially on ruled notebook paper," he said.

"Probably not," she admitted.

"You know, we really should divide up the coins," Will told her. "If that note was about the coins, someone knows you have them."

Rachel looked uncomfortable.

"I promise not to take them to California, Rachel."

She really couldn't argue with him. If they couldn't put the coins in a safe deposit box, the next best thing was to divide them. "Not here. Someone could see."

Will got up and extended a hand to Rachel. He pulled her to her feet. "Come on. I know a place we can go. It's behind the gardening shed. I found another shed back in the sea roses. No one will see us there."

****

"How should we divide them?" Will asked.

Rachel sat down on a rock by the shed and opened the pouch. She poured the four coins out into her left hand. "We'll each pick one and go back and forth."

Will nodded. "You go first. You found them."

Rachel already knew the one she wanted. "I want the French coin," she said and lifted the coin from among the others. "You know, we still don't know too much about this coin."

Will studied the remaining coins in Rachel's hand. He turned each one over methodically.

"You don't have to take all day," Rachel complained.

"Okay, okay." He turned each one over again as Rachel rolled her eyes.

"I want the oldest one," he announced, and took the 1694 copper coin.

Rachel immediately took another coin. "I want the 1708 coin with the woman's face." She handed the remaining coin to Will.

"What about the pouch?" Will asked her.

"What about it?"

"Well, you've had it for a while and I was thinking that…" He looked at her hopefully, but didn't finish the sentence.

"Oh, all right." She handed Will the leather pouch.

He instantly slipped his two coins inside and closed it. Will shoved it into his pocket. "Let me see that note again."

Will took the note and studied it for a moment. "How do you even know this was meant for you?" Will rationalized. "Maybe it was for Steve."

Rachel hadn't thought of that.

Chapter Eleven

Rachel walked slowly towad the wharf about two steps behind Will. She knew they needed to talk to Old Jake, but wasn't in any hurry. If anyone could give them information on The Scot, it would be him. But why couldn't they wait until morning? Old Jake's boat hadn't been at the wharf when they arrived shortly after 7:00. Now it was getting dark. This was just like television. People always choosing nighttime to go to the scariest places in the world. In Rachel's mind, Old Jake's was definitely one of those places.

"Old Jake creeps me out," Will admitted as they walked away from the crowded section of the boardwalk and toward the deserted wharf.

Rachel knew exactly what Will meant. Old Jake had been a fisherman in the area for as long as Rachel could remember.

He knew everything about Olde Locke Beach and The Isles of Shoals.

Unfortunately, Old Jake was mean. Once, when he was telling stories to some of the lobstermen's kids, she got so scared she ran away. Her brother, Steve, didn't catch up with her until she was almost halfway home. Even though that happened four years before, when she was eight, it seemed like yesterday.

The boardwalk was less active the further down they walked. They were almost at the end of the boardwalk and entering the wharf when Rachel spotted them. It was the two teenage boys. Rachel grabbed Will's arm and swung him around to face her.

"They're coming this way!"

"Who?"

"Those guys…those boys…!"

"Where?"

Rachel's eyes were riveted on the boys. They were walking toward Rachel and Will and she didn't want a confrontation.

The boys were just about upon them. Will's back was to them, but Rachel could watch as the boys moved toward them.

One was slightly taller than the other. Perhaps he was a bit older, Rachel thought. Both had light brown hair that probably used to be blond. Their features were similar, round faces and large noses.

They were just about to pass Rachel and Will when the taller one leaned his shoulder into Will as they passed.

"Hey!" Will shouted as he stumbled forward into Rachel. He was just about to take off after them when Rachel blocked his way. "Let it go!" She could see the anger in Will's eyes. "They're each a whole head taller than you!"

"Jerk!" Will called out.

Now Will could see them in the streetlight. "Whoa! Maybe they're *two* heads taller!" She saw the sparkle in his eyes.

"You definitely told them!" she said as she pushed him in the direction of the pier. Will did not resist.

The wharf was empty. During the day, it would be bustling. They found Old Jake aboard his fishing boat. A small lantern provided an eerie light. He was working at untangling a net. He didn't even look up at them when he asked, "What do you two want?"

"Uh..." Rachel felt like she was eight again. "We wondered if you would tell us what you know about the pirates in the area."

Jake looked at them now. His white beard glistened in the faint light cast by his lantern. The weathered lines in his face were deep. "Who do you want to know about?"

Will spoke. "The Scot."

"'The Scot!' Well, I'll be..." Jake stopped in mid-sentence.

"Not too many folks know about The Scot. His real name was Sandy Gordon."

"Was he bloodthirsty like Blackbeard?" Will asked.

"Well, he was a crazy one...absolutely ruthless."

"What does ruthless mean?" Will asked.

Old Jake sat back. "Ruthless? Well, let's see, ruthless means somebody who doesn't care about anyone, somebody who's cruel."

Old Jake smiled and leaned forward. He looked right into Will's eyes. "Sandy Gordon once burned a man's eyes out with a poker!"

Will's eyes widened to the size of saucers as he leaned away from Old Jake's face.

Old Jake smiled again. But it wasn't a friendly smile. It was a self-satisfied smirk. Rachel could tell that Old Jake enjoyed frightening them. She remembered when she had run away and wondered if Old Jake had the same satisfied look then. She felt her face getting hot and knew she was blushing. She wasn't about to let Old Jake scare her away this time.

Rachel asked, "When did Sandy Gordon live around here?"

Old Jake hesitated, then said, "Well, that would be at the same time as Blackbeard."

Will piped up, "They knew each other, didn't they?"

Old Jake nodded. "They pirated together for a spell."

Will sat down on an upside-down pail as Old Jake spoke.

"Sandy Gordon was from Glasgow. That's in Scotland."

"The Scot!" Will said. He turned to Rachel and said, "That's why they called him The Scot!"

Jake nodded. "He was a real troublemaker, if you know what I mean. Spent a good deal of time in the Glasgow jail." Jake worked on the net as he spoke.

"One day he was hanging around the docks and was offered a job aboard a boat that was shipping out. Sandy fell into his old ways soon after setting sail and before too long he was stealing from his fellow shipmates. Well, the captain didn't like Sandy much and thought he might be the one causing trouble on the ship. And," he said with a wink to Will, "good ole Sandy started hanging around the captain's daughter who was also on the ship."

"Why was she on board?" Will asked.

"Can't say that I know. But, what I do know is that the captain caught the two of them in her cabin one night!" Old Jake shook his head. "Well, that was all the captain needed to go after Sandy. He tied him to the mainsail and gave him one hundred lashes!"

"Whoa! That could kill a guy!" Will said, and gave a long drawn-out whistle.

Old Jake grimaced and continued, "Well, Sandy Gordon

spent thirty days in the ship's brig and during that time planned his revenge. You see, there were other sailors who had suffered at the hand of the captain and Sandy knew it. When he got out of the brig, he got his revenge."

"How?" Will asked.

"Only three days after Sandy was out of the brig, it happened. Sandy Gordon and some fellow mutineers tied the captain to the mast and gave him a hundred lashes.

"When they cut him down, Sandy Gordon burned both of the captain's eyes out with a burning hot poker and threw him overboard!" Old Jake slapped Will on the shoulder, a grin the size of a merchant ship on his face. Will, on the other hand, looked a little green.

Will gathered his wits and asked, "Is that when Sandy Gordon came to the Isles of Shoals?"

"No. He and the others traveled along the coast of Europe and Britain pirating. But Sandy wasn't one for sharing. They say he stole millions in treasure, but didn't give much to his crew. So, the mutineers set Sandy adrift off the coast of Scotland.

"Well, Sandy Gordon lived alone in an abandoned farmhouse for a very long time. But, one afternoon he spied a ship, way out in the distance. Finally, the ship came in to the bay and dropped anchor and several men came ashore. The men were looking for water and Sandy showed them where they could find some."

"Is that when he met Blackbeard?" Will asked again.

Old Jake nodded. "Yep. Sandy Gordon was introduced to Edward Teach."

Will looked over at Rachel. "That's Blackbeard. His real name was Edward Teach."

"I know, I know."

"Sandy told Blackbeard about all of his days as a pirate and asked if Blackbeard would take him along."

"So he did, right?" Will asked.

Old Jake nodded again. "Blackbeard told him he would give Sandy a chance, but if he failed he would be killed. Old Sandy showed his worth. Blackbeard gave him a Spanish ship they had captured and Sandy named it *The Flying Scot.*

"Sandy set out on his own and was very successful as a pirate. He sailed off the European coast and folks say he ended up with a treasure worth millions."

"Wow!" Rachel couldn't help herself.

"That's when Sandy Gordon decided to come to America and settle in. He picked White Island, right off the coast here."

"Why would he pick this place?" Rachel questioned.

"Easy to spot the enemy," Old Jake answered.

Rachel and Will exchanged nods.

"So, Sandy built a cabin and buried his fortune right on White Island. From there he ran raids when he felt like it. However, after about a year or so, he heard that the British were searching for pirates in the area."

"Uh oh!" Will said.

Old Jake nodded again. "One morning he saw a fleet of British ships headed his way. He tried to ready *The Flying Scot* to leave, but by the time she was ready to set sail, the British ships were too close."

Old Jake took a deep breath. "Sandy had no choice but to fight. But when it was clear he was going to lose the battle, you know what he did?"

Wide-eyed, they both shook their heads no.

"Sandy grabbed a burning torch and set the gun powder on the ship on fire!"

"No!" Will shouted.

"Yes!" Jake laughed. "The ship exploded and Sandy and all of his men were killed instantly. In those days they hanged pirates. Sandy had nothing to lose."

"What about the treasure?" Will asked.

"No one was alive to tell about it. To this day, it's never been found."

****

The boardwalk was almost deserted when they left Old Jake.

The humid breeze smelled of salt and the waves lapped softly along the shoreline. The Atlantic seldom had strong waves, except during a storm. Rachel and Will walked along the boardwalk.

Rachel was trying to make sense of what Old Jake had told them when Will asked, "Do you think the coins drifted into shore from the explosion?" Will asked the question Rachel had been pondering.

Rachel shook her head, "I guess it's possible. In some ways it makes a lot of sense that some of his treasure washed up on shore."

Will agreed. "Yeah," he paused, "I guess treasure from The Scot is as good as treasure from Blackbeard. But I was kind of hoping for Blackbeard. Who's heard of The Scot?"

At that moment, Rachel thought she heard something. She reached for Will's arm and rested her hand on top of his wrist. As Will turned to look at her, she put a finger to her lips to signal him to be quiet.

He was. They stopped and listened.

The waves continued to lap softly against the sand.

Nothing else was heard.

Will suddenly grabbed Rachel's shoulders.

"What?" she whispered. "Do you hear something?"

Will's eyes were wide and he spoke in a slow whisper. "I think it's Sandy Gordon! Listen Rachel…I think I can hear him." He shook her by the shoulders. "He's saying, 'I want my money! I want my money!'"

Rachel whirled around. "Stop it, Will!" she demanded. "That's not funny!" She pulled his hands from her shoulders in disgust. "You're such a jerk!"

Rachel was angry. She had just confided in him about seeing a ghost and now he was making fun of her. Why was it that she was afraid he would leave? Right now she thought it wasn't a bad idea.

"I'm getting a drink of water," she told him. Rachel walked around the corner of the information center building toward the drinking fountain located next to the public restroom. She took a drink, but when she lifted her head, she was grabbed by her tee shirt and thrown through the swinging bathroom door. The door swung closed and Rachel found herself alone.

"Will! You jerk!" she shouted. She tried to push the door open. She budged the door a little, but not enough to free her.

"Will, cut it out!" she shouted at the top of her lungs. "This isn't funny!"

Sometimes Will's sense of humor left a lot to be desired. She tried the door again. It was still blocked. She tried kicking it—nothing!

The restrooms usually stayed open until 10:00 p.m., and it wasn't 10:00 yet. She looked around. Rachel had been in this restroom at least a hundred times, but had never really paid any attention to the inside. More importantly, she had never looked to see if there was a window.

Rachel kicked the door again, but this time it swung open effortlessly. She lunged out the door. "Will! Where are you, you big dumb dope!" She spun around ready for his attack this time. Or ready to attack him.

"Will!" she called out again.

He didn't answer. Now what was he doing? Hiding from her? Given her anger level, it probably wasn't a bad idea. "Will!" she yelled at the top of her lungs.

Rachel heard what sounded like a moan. She listened again.

"Will?" Rachel shouted again.

This time she heard his voice: "Why'd you hit me over the head?"

Rachel ran over to where she had left Will. He sat on the cement walkway by the railing rubbing his head. "That wasn't funny."

"Will...I..."

"I knew you were mad...but that hurt! Then, when you

pushed me, or tripped me, or whatever, I hit my head on the railing."

A railing divided the sandy beach from the boardwalk.

Rachel reached out to help him up, but he wouldn't take her hand.

"Get lost."

Rachel knew he was getting madder by the moment. "Will, I didn't hit you, or push you, or trip you. I wouldn't do that. Somebody shoved me into the bathroom and held the door closed. I thought it was you!"

"Yeah, right! It must have been a ghost!"

"Will, I'm not kidding!" Now Rachel was getting angry. "I would never do that to you!"

He looked up at her, still rubbing his head. "Yeah?"

"Yeah!" she shouted at him. "Did you see anyone?" Rachel asked as she looked around.

He shook his head no. "Ouch!" He cringed after shaking it. "No, did you?"

"No."

Rachel looked out over the black water. "I don't like this."

Will tried to make sense of what happened. "You know, I probably just tripped."

"You think?" Rachel looked at him uneasily, "So who held the door shut so I couldn't get out of the bathroom?"

Will shrugged.

Suddenly, it came to her. "Will! Check your pocket. Do you still have the coins?"

Will was on his feet in a flash. He reached into the front pocket of his jeans. "They're gone!" Even in the darkening shadows, Rachel could see the look of horror on his face.

"Maybe they just fell out of your pocket," Rachel said hopefully.

They crawled around on the cement pavement. The light was poor, so it was difficult to see. After several minutes, they stopped looking.

"They're gone!" Will said, sinking back down on the cement. "Now my head really hurts."

"Maybe we should go to the police!" Rachel said.

"What are we going to tell the police?" Will asked.

Chapter Twelve

Rachel arrived at the Isles View Hotel shortly after 9:00 a.m. Will was already working.

"How do you feel?" Rachel asked, circling him.

"Better than last night."

"We need a plan," Rachel said.

"Yeah, no kidding. But, we need one that won't land us in jail!" Will retorted. "I can see that look in your eyes that always means trouble."

Rachel rolled her eyes. "Don't be so dramatic!" she told him. "We need to get inside and check out some of the rooms that overlook the rocks."

"I don't know." Will hesitated.

"Will, someone knocked you down and stole our coins."

"I know." He looked around. "And I want to catch the guy

who did it, but…"

Rachel stepped away from the building and looked up at the bank of windows of the three-story hotel. "We need to see who's staying in the rooms that have a view of the beach. We keep talking about the people on the beach, but what about the people who could *see* the beach?"

Will looked skeptical. "How do we do it without getting arrested?"

Rachel smiled. "Our pet care service. The Isles View Hotel allows pets."

Rachel and Will entered the hotel lobby through the side door. They hoped they could get upstairs without being caught by Barb or Ben. They knew that only three rooms on the second and third floors could have views of the rock formation where the coins were discovered. They also knew the one lower unit rented by Khaki Man and Hat Lady had a clear view of the rocks. The rest of the first floor was where Ben and Barb lived.

"We probably should have put away the gardening equipment," Will lamented. "If Ben goes outside, he's going to have an attack. Maybe I should…"

"Oh no you don't." Rachel grabbed his wrist as he turned to walk away. "We'll be back at work in just a few minutes." Then she whispered, "We'll start at the top floor first and work our way down."

"Why?" he asked.

"I don't know," she answered.

Will rolled his eyes, but followed her.

Just as they reached the bottom of the staircase, Will looked over at a small table. "Hey!" he exclaimed, grabbing something from the table. "Look at this. These are coupons!"

"Shh!" Rachel looked around to see who was watching.

In the small room off the lobby, Rachel saw the backs of the two teenaged girls she had seen leaving the beach when she arrived with Greta. The mother sat facing the doorway, but seemed to be arguing with the girls. She was clearly not paying any attention to Rachel and Will.

Will continued, "These are coupons for the ferry to the Isles of Shoals. Two for one! We could have saved fifteen dollars!"

Rachel looked at the paper in his hand. "Well, now we know why so many people were on the ferry."

Will gave her a disgusted look. "Who cares about that? We could have saved fifteen bucks!"

Rachel patted Will on the arm sympathetically. "Water under the bridge," she told him. "Come on."

"I think I might get sick!" Will complained. "Fifteen bucks!"

Rachel turned to him. "Get a grip!"

Will stuffed the coupon into his pocket and followed Rachel up the stairs.

When they reached the top floor, Will reached out to knock on the first door. Rachel stopped him. "We need a plan," she told him. "We can't just…"

Suddenly, the door swung open and Rachel and Will found themselves eyeball to eyeball with a dark-haired man who looked like he could use a shave and a comb. "What are you two doing outside my door?" he demanded.

So much for a plan, Rachel thought. "Uh…we have a pet service and were wondering if you needed our help." Rachel took the opportunity to lean into the room and look around. "Do you have any pets?" she asked him.

Will's eyes searched the room too, as he stood on his toes to glance out the side window.

The man's eyes narrowed. "What are you kids up to?"

"Nothing!" Rachel sounded as innocent as she could.

The man slammed the door, nearly smacking her in the head.

Will grabbed Rachel's elbow and pulled her away from the door. "We'd better do this fast. I'm afraid he might call down-stairs to the desk and tell Ben or Barb about us."

"Right. I'll take this floor and you take the second floor and we'll meet outside."

Will sprinted to the stairs.

Rachel knocked on the next door. A young woman with long red hair answered. Next to her stood a little red-haired girl in her pajamas. "Yes?" The woman asked.

Rachel gave her sales pitch, but the young woman informed her that they had not brought a pet with them. Rachel was able to see slightly into the room. It looked like a hurricane had hit. There were toys and clothes all over the floor. Just then, a little red-haired boy peeked around the door.

"Do you baby-sit?" the woman asked hopefully.

"Uh, no. Pets only," Rachel managed as she backed away from the door. "Thanks for your time."

"Do you know of anyone?" the woman asked as Rachel was trying to get away.

Rachel shook her head, no. "Sorry," she told her as she started toward the next room.

The woman pulled both children inside and closed the door.

"I'll scratch her off the list as a suspect," Rachel said aloud as she walked to the next room. "She has no time to bother with us."

Rachel knocked on the third door. No answer. She then made her way downstairs as quickly as possible. When she reached the bottom floor, she glanced around. Neither Ben nor Barb was in sight. Rachel slipped out the side door to wait for Will.

****

"Rachel!" Will looked wildly around to be sure no one was watching. "What are you doing?"

Rachel had propped her hoe up against the weathered shingles of the beachfront hotel and was peering into the window of Khaki Man and Hat Lady's rented room. She now raised her hands and cupped them against the glass to cut out the glare. "I'm trying to see inside," she said, not turning around.

Will looked around again and darted over to her side. He pulled one of her hands away from the glass. "Are you crazy?"

She pulled her hand away from his and cupped it back onto the glass. "Will, you have to see this." She turned and grabbed his hand pulling him closer to the window.

Now it was Will's turn to pull his hand away from hers. "No! You're going to get us fired!"

She kept peering through the glass. "This room had a perfect view of the rocks where we found the coins." She leaned closer. "Will... look!"

"Rachel!" Will said again. "Forget about being fired. You're going to get us arrested!"

She turned and faced him. "You have to look at what's..." She suddenly stopped speaking.

Khaki Man rounded the corner of the building. Her eyes lifted from Will's and widened as they met the man's eyes. His eyes were steel blue and not in the least bit friendly looking.

"What's all this about being arrested?" Khaki Man boomed.

Will jumped and shifted closer to Rachel. Normally she would have laughed at him for being startled, but there was nothing funny about it now.

Rachel and Will stood shoulder to shoulder staring at Khaki Man. Neither of them spoke.

The man's eyes remained fixed on them. "Well?"

Rachel stammered, "Uh, he just means that…the terrible job we're doing… someone could arrest us." She reached for the hoe propped up against the side of the building, but missed, knocking it down amongst the low bushes that surrounded the structure.

Will took the opportunity to continue with the story. "Yeah," Will agreed. "She's doing a really lousy job."

Rachel wanted to elbow Will, but didn't.

The man took a step toward them as he demanded, "What are you kids doing here?"

"We work here," Rachel said, with more confidence.

Will chimed in, "Yeah, we do yard work here at the hotel." He bent down to pick up the fallen hoe.

The man asked, "Do the owners pay you to snoop in guest's rooms?"

"No, uh…," Rachel stammered, "I was working." She pointed to the hoe. "And I thought I might have cracked the glass and I…" She could feel sweat pouring down her back.

"Yeah, well we'd better get back to work," Will said as he nudged Rachel forward. They didn't stop moving until they were out of hearing range of Khaki Man.

"You're out of your mind!" Will griped once they were out of earshot. "What do you think you were doing?"

Rachel looked back towards Khaki Man. He still stood in the same spot, watching them.

"Will, I saw something on the table."

"What?"

She looked back, again, at Khaki Man, who was still looking at them. "There were coins on the table!"

Will's mouth dropped open. "Do you think…?"

He didn't have a chance to finish his question.

Rachel interrupted, "Khaki Man and Hat Lady were following us out at the Isles of Shoals. I thought so, then, but I'm sure of it now!"

Will was angry. "They were probably the ones who hit me over the head and stole our coins." He rubbed his head.

"And," Rachel added, "they probably followed me the other night."

"But how do we prove it?" Will asked.

"Tonight," she told him. "We'll come back tonight and prove it."

Chapter Thirteen

Will looked at his watch as he walked through the door of his house. It was 7:40 p.m. He was supposed to meet Rachel at her house at 8:00. After he and his father had dinner, he had gone over to Mr. Clement's house to mow the lawn. Mr. Clement lived three houses down and had hired Will every summer since he was eight years old.

It should only have taken a half hour, but at the last minute, Mr. Clement decided he wanted Will to plant flowers in the pots by the front door and in the flowerbed along the front walkway. He gave Will a ten dollar bill and said Will was a great sport to agree to plant them.

Will wasn't sure when he agreed to do the extra work, but he smiled at Mr. Clement as he pocketed the extra ten dollars. Ten dollars didn't seem too bad until Will saw how many weeds had grown in the flowerbed. They would have to be pulled before he could plant the flowers.

The jobs always seemed to take longer than he planned, especially when the client paid by the job instead of by the hour. He decided he should talk to Rachel about a way to make sure they were getting paid the right amount of money. Of course, when they were paid by the hour, the client sometimes complained they weren't working fast enough.

"Dad?" Will called out as he came through the door. "I'm home!"

"I'm in the den."

Will worked his way towards the den, stopping at the cookie jar on the kitchen counter. He removed three cookies and shoved one into his mouth before reaching the den doorway. "Did Mom call? She said she would call early."

Mr. Reynolds did not look up from the pile of papers on his desk. "About twenty minutes ago."

"I got held up at the job," Will mumbled. His mouth was full of cookies. "Should I call her back? Did she say when she wants me to come out?"

Still not looking up, his father replied, "Work it out with her."

Will sighed audibly. He knew they had probably argued over the phone. If he had been home and taken the call, maybe...

Will turned and started to walk away when his father stopped him. "That little friend of yours called. She said to meet her at the Isles View Hotel lobby right away." Mr. Reynolds now looked up. "Will, she was quite rude on the phone. She just said to tell you to hurry. I don't like…"

"When did she call?"

"Just before your mother."

"I've got to go!"

"Will, what about your mother?"

Will was already halfway to the side door as he yelled back, "I'll call her later!"

Will was more than a little surprised that Rachel had called and changed their plans. He knew she wanted to check out Khaki Man and Hat Lady's room, but he thought they were going to talk about how they were going to do it together. He had planned to go to her house after he cleaned up.

Will jumped on his bike, popped on his helmet, and took off down the quiet residential street. When he reached Ocean Road, he turned left and pedaled toward the Isles View Hotel. It wasn't dark yet. The sea breeze was light and the ocean was calm. Will hoped Rachel hadn't done anything foolish without him, and he hoped she hadn't planned anything foolish to do with him.

Will rode into the parking area of the Isles View Hotel, got off his bike and walked it to the far side of the hotel. He pushed the bike into the sea roses. Ben had hollered at him once before about leaving his bike in the way of the guests. It wouldn't be in anyone's way here, he reasoned.

Will looked around the parking area, but didn't see Rachel. He entered the hotel through the front door and walked through the lobby. No sign of her.

Will stood in the small lobby and was just about to sit down to wait when he saw Khaki Man and Hat Lady sitting in a small adjoining room. He turned to go outside to wait for Rachel.

It was then that he noticed an envelope propped up on the lobby counter with the word "Will" printed on the front. Will picked up the envelope, opened it, and pulled out a piece of paper. He looked at the paper, turned it over to see the other side, and looked around the lobby. Then he put the note and envelope into his pocket and walked out the back door of the Isles View Hotel.

Chapter Fourteen

The phone rang outside of Rachel's bedroom. She shared a phone line with Steve, but most of the calls were for her. The handset lay on the floor. Rachel looked at her watch. It was 8:35 p.m. She rolled forward on the area rug and picked it up. Maybe it was Will. He was late.

"Will?" she said as she hit the talk button.

There was a crackling on the other end.

"Will, is that you?" Rachel waited. "Will? I can hardly hear you. The connection is bad, I..."

Then a muffled voice cut her off, "*Put...them...back*!" the voice told her.

"What? Who is this?" Rachel demanded.

"*Put...them...back...if you want to see your friend again*!"

"Who is this?" Rachel demanded again.

The voice responded speaking slowly, in a halting manner, *"Don't...tell...anyone! Put...them...back where you found them...at 9:00 tonight! Go home...immediately after!"* Then there was a click and the line went dead.

Rachel sprung up from the floor, her mind racing. "My friend!" she said aloud. She felt her stomach drop as she said, "Will!"

Rachel instinctively hit Will's number on the speed dial. She looked at her watch. It was 8:36. It would take twenty minutes to bike to the Isles View Hotel. Her heart and head were pounding in unison.

The line connected. "Hello?"

"Will, Will, is that you?"

"No."

Rachel now knew it was Mr. Reynolds. She wished she had listened more carefully when he first answered the telephone. Too late now, she had to stay calm. "Is Will there?" She tried to keep her voice low and steady.

"Who is this?" Mr. Reynolds asked. There was an irritated edge to his voice.

"This is Rachel. I need to talk to Will." She paused and added, "Please."

Mr. Reynolds let out a sigh. "Rachel, I already gave him your message. Didn't he meet you?"

"What message?"

Rachel heard Mr. Reynolds let out another long sigh.

"The message you gave me an hour ago." Mr. Reynolds was clearly exasperated.

"What message was that?" Rachel asked trying hard not to sound upset or stupid. She didn't want to tip off Mr. Reynolds that she was worried, at least not yet. She needed time to think. The voice had said, don't tell anyone.

"Rachel, is this some sort of game? I'm not in the mood to play games with you children."

Now Rachel felt irritated, but didn't let on. "No, I just forgot where I asked him to meet me." She lied.

Mr. Reynolds accepted the response. "You said to meet you at the Isles View Hotel lobby."

Rachel was silent.

"Rachel, is there something wrong?" He suddenly sounded less exasperated and more concerned.

In her head she could hear the words, *Don't...tell...anyone.* Then she heard herself say, "No, I just uh…"

"Rachel, are you sure everything is all right?"

"Yeah, uh, I'd better get going!" She hung up quickly.

She felt dizzy. What should she do? Should she tell Mr. Reynolds? Should she call the police? But what would she tell them? She didn't know what was going on herself. The voice warned her not to tell anyone. And the voice gave her only twenty minutes.

The voice. It was muffled, distorted, unreal. Maybe the caller had covered the receiver. Rachel was certain of one thing, the caller sounded female.

"*Put...them...back.*" That's all the voice said she had to do. If she put the coins back, Will would be safe.

Rachel grabbed the chair from her desk and dragged it across the hardwood floor causing a screeching sound. She opened her closet door and climbed onto the chair, reaching to the upper shelf where she pulled down an old Barbie doll case.

Then she dropped off the chair with a loud thud and knelt down on the floor. Rachel rummaged through old Barbie doll clothes and accessories she hadn't played with in a long time, tossing them all over. She had placed the coins here after Will's coins were stolen. No one would think to look in an old Barbie doll case, she reasoned.

She found them, the 1708 silver coin and the French coin. Rachel pocketed the coins, bounded down the stairs, and headed for the kitchen door.

"Hey, slow down." Mrs. Clark was studying at the kitchen table. She reached out and grabbed the end of Rachel's sweatshirt as she tried to make her way out the side door. The sweatshirt stretched, but Mrs. Clark's grip won out.

"I've got to meet Will!"

"Now?" Mrs. Clark searched Rachel's face. "What's the rush?"

"I'm late!" Rachel met her mother's eyes with a steady gaze. She was telling the truth. She had to meet Will, well sort of, and she was late.

Mrs. Clark let go of the sweatshirt. "It's 8:40."

Rachel said, "I'll be back by 9:00." It was a lie. She knew she wouldn't be back until after 9:00. Her heart was beating so hard, she was sure her mother could hear it.

Mrs. Clark narrowed her eyes, but then she nodded.

****

Rachel was on her bike in seconds flat and riding full speed down her street toward Ocean Road. The sun had already set, but there was still light in the sky. If her mother had known she was riding her bike so far in the rapidly dimming light, she never would have allowed it. The bike had a light and reflectors, but a driver would find her difficult to see, especially since Rachel was wearing a dark sweatshirt.

She slowed at each intersection as she headed down to the beach, but never stopped. Fortunately, there was never much traffic on the residential streets. Once she hit Ocean Road, it would change. It would definitely be crowded with cars. But, at least there were streetlights that would help a driver see her.

The caller had given her no time to think. She tried to come up with a plan as she rode, but her thoughts were jumbled and confused. None of this made any sense to her. The kidnapper would have to retrieve the coins. Where could she hide to catch the kidnapper? Would Will be safer if she tackled the kidnapper? Would Will be safer if she just did what was demanded?

Rachel wanted to race up to the caller and tackle her. Then, when she was on the ground, demand to know where Will was. No, she reasoned. She should stay concealed and watch to see who picked up the coins. She now knew the caller was not one of the teenage boys, or at least it was unlikely. But, if the caller was Hat Lady, Khaki Man would be close by.

****

Rachel was gasping for breath as she reached the Isles View Hotel. She hadn't coasted her bike once since she left her house and she felt as if her lungs might explode. She skidded to a stop at the far side of the hotel and immediately dropped her bike onto a sandy patch along the beach side of the road.

From here, she would hide in the overgrowth of sea roses to watch for whoever was coming for the coins. It wasn't the best spot. It was the *only* spot. It would have to do.

Rachel ran back to the paved entrance to the Isles View Hotel. When she reached the entrance, she deliberately slowed down so she wouldn't draw attention to herself. Then she walked down the driveway and on to the stone path that led to the small private beach. She passed the hotel itself, crossed the lawn and moved on to the sand.

No one was out on the sand at this time of night and there were no lights illuminating the sand. A thick blanket of clouds kept the moonlight at bay.

Rachel felt a chill shiver down her spine. Up until this moment she had only thought about Will and what he might be going through. Suddenly, she was concerned for herself. Someone could easily come up behind her or be waiting for her by the rock formation. Will's bump on the head was still very fresh in her mind.

The lapping waves would make it impossible to hear anyone. She crossed the sand, constantly turning to look behind her.

Rachel reached the rocks, moved to the ocean side of the formation and placed the two coins onto the sand. Looking at the hotel she whispered, "Whoever you are, you'd better get these coins in the next fifteen minutes or they will be washed away." The tide was dangerously close.

Rachel paused to steal a glance at the hotel windows. She didn't want to be obvious, but couldn't resist a quick look. She immediately thought better of the idea and turned her gaze back to the sea. Someone could be watching with binoculars. All she wanted was for Will to be safe.

She stood up, dusted the sand off of her hands and walked back towards the parking lot and street. Rachel kept her head down pretending to watch the sand where she walked. But she couldn't help turning her eyes upward, peering again into the windows of the hotel. There were several rooms with lights on. Some had the blinds open, some not. Rachel couldn't see anyone watching her.

She reached the building just as a couple came out of the side door. For a moment, she thought it was Khaki Man and Hat Lady, but as she passed them she knew it wasn't.

Rachel walked slowly through the parking lot toward the street, wanting to see where the couple was going. They went to a car parked in the lot. Rachel watched until the engine started and the car pulled away, then she made her way back to the road and her bike. All she could do now was wait for the caller to retrieve the coins and free Will.

Rachel rolled her bike off the side of the road and pushed it through the sea rose bushes that bordered the street. The bushes crackled as she moved through, scratching her skin. She pushed them aside and continued until she found a spot where she could see the rock formation. Unfortunately, she was not able to see the back of the hotel. She settled. It was the best she could do.

Rachel looked up at the sky. The heavy cloud cover remained. If the bank of clouds didn't move through quickly, Rachel knew it would be difficult, if not impossible, to see who picked up the coins. All she could do was wait.

Rachel had only been waiting for a few minutes, but it seemed like an eternity. The sound of the waves breaking became louder and Rachel worried that the coins could be swept away. She had resisted the urge to go get them, but it was getting more and more difficult to wait. Where was the caller? More importantly, where was Will? If the coins were swept away, would the female voice release Will?

Cars whizzed by on the road heading north up the coast. Rachel started to count them. One, two came close together. There was a lag and then three, four and five, sped by her. At one hundred, she would go and get the coins, she decided. When she reached seventy-three, she thought she saw some movement on the sand near the rock formation.

Rachel rose to her knees and searched the sand with her eyes. Faint moonlight now broke through the clouds and Rachel was able to make out a form. Something about the size of the form and the way it moved suggested to Rachel that it was a woman. She was dressed in white. Rachel caught a glimpse of yellow in the moonlight.

Rachel moved forward in the bushes as far as she could while still remaining hidden from sight. From here, she watched the form bend down over the sand where Rachel had placed the two remaining coins. Rachel knew her heart should have been pounding, but the sight wasn't at all frightening. The figure was graceful and seemed strangely peaceful. But suddenly, as quickly as she had appeared, the figure was gone. Rachel looked around frantically.

Her mind now raced. What if she had handled the situation wrong? Should she have called the police? Where is Will?

She looked up at the sky. The moonlight was filtering through the clouds, bright enough to be able to see a figure on the sand. Rachel stood up and scanned the beach. Nothing. No one. Fear began to grip her. Now she had no chance of identifying the figure. If anything happened to Will she would never forgive herself. She had to run down to the beach. She took two steps, but stopped herself. No, she couldn't panic now, she told herself. She had given the coins back as the caller demanded. Will should be released unharmed. She should go home like the caller told her.

Rachel stepped back into the shrubs and was about to go

back to her bike when she suddenly saw another form moving toward the rock formation. Rachel crouched down and watched. This form, dressed in darker clothing, somehow seemed female. Whoever it was stood by the rocks for a moment, looking warily around, then ducked down. In a few moments, the figure emerged from the rocks and again scanned the beach, then ran across the sand toward the hotel. Rachel lost sight of the mysterious figure as it moved behind the building.

Chapter Fifteen

Rachel checked her e-mail for the millionth time. She knew it was silly. She knew Will would call or come over once he was free, but she checked the e-mail anyway. Maybe there would be a message from him. There wasn't. Rachel glanced at the time. It was 10:46 p.m. At 11:00, she told herself, she would do something. But what? She held the phone in one hand as she walked to the window and looked outside.

When Rachel had returned home, her mom had been busy studying in the dining room. Fortunately, there was no clock in that room and Mrs. Clark rarely wore a watch. Rachel quickly said goodnight and went to her room before any curfew questions were asked. But, after sitting in her room for close to an hour, holding the phone in her hand, staring at it, willing it to ring, she decided to go downstairs and sit in the den and wait.

Her parents and brother were already in bed. Having to get up at the crack of dawn to go lobstering resulted in a lights-out policy at 10:00 p.m. at her house. Rachel moved away from the window and back to the computer. She checked for messages once more. Nothing.

Rachel picked up a pen laying next to a yellow pad and jotted down the dates of the coins, 1694 and 1698. Those were the coins that were stolen. Then she wrote 1708 and L'AN 12. Did they belong to Blackbeard or Sandy Gordon? Did a ghost protect them? Rachel couldn't shake the image of the first figure that visited the rock formation. The thought should have sent shivers down Rachel's spine then, or now, but it didn't. Just as it had while she watched, the memory of the figure of the woman in white had a calming effect.

Rachel hit the quit button and closed her e-mail. As soon as she did, an internet encyclopedia site appeared on her screen. Rachel figured Steve had been using it.

It was one of those sites that listed the alphabet and all she had to do was to click on the letter. Rachel had been planning to check on the coin from the French Revolution. Now was as good a time as any. She moved the cursor to "F" for French Revolution and clicked.

Rachel glanced at her watch again and waited for the information to come up on the screen. The search name flashed and listed choices that were further alphabetized within the letter "F". She selected "Fran-Fre" and smiled. Mr. Barnes, her third grade teacher, had made them alphabetize spelling and vocabulary words every week. At the time, she thought it was a useless skill, but he always insisted that one day it would come in handy. He was right. Today was the day. Rachel looked at her watch again and tapped the desk nervously. The listing of entries appeared on the screen and Rachel quickly scrolled down the list until she found "French Revolution" and clicked the mouse.

Rachel looked at the screen. She blinked and leaned forward, just to be sure she was actually seeing what she thought she was seeing. The first sentence read: "The French Revolution began in 1789."

"1789!" Rachel knew the coin was dated AN 12 or L'An 12. If L'An 1 was after 1789, then... Her mind raced as she tried to sort through the new information. If the coins were from Blackbeard's or Sandy Gordon's treasure and the pirates were at the Shoals during 1716 to 1717, then how was it possible that they had a coin dated near 1800?

The answer was simple. It wasn't possible. The realization made Rachel dizzy. She and Will had been so caught up in the belief it was pirates' treasure they never found the date of the last coin. This changed everything.

Rachel was still trying to make sense of all of this when the phone rang. She hit the talk button halfway through the first ring. "Will?"

A female voice demanded, "*Where's... the...other...coin?*"

"What?" Rachel was stunned.

"*Put...the...other...coin...back...now!*"

"I don't know what you're talking about!" Rachel tried to explain. "I put the coins back!"

Rachel tried to think, but she was finding it nearly impossible. What was going on? What was she supposed to do? Who was this voice on the phone?

"I put both coins back!" Rachel tried desperately to convince the voice.

"*Liar! Put...it...back! You have one half-hour...if you want to see your friend again!*"

"Okay! Okay!" Rachel stalled. She knew the caller didn't believe her. "But I need more time!"

There was silence on the other end of the line.

Rachel looked at her watch. It was almost 11:00. The voice demanded the coin be returned in one half-hour. That would be 11:30. She needed more time, but knew she couldn't push it too far. "Midnight!" Rachel nearly shouted. "I'll put it back at midnight!"

The voice didn't answer.

"Midnight!" Rachel pleaded. "Please give me until midnight! That was the problem before! I didn't have enough time to get the other coin!"

"*Midnight*! *No...Police*! *No...Tricks*!" the voice demanded. Then the line went dead.

****

Rachel pedaled as fast as she could to Ocean Road. She made a left turn when she reached the beach and headed north. The muscles in her legs burned as she pedaled, but she didn't let up. Rachel touched her sweatshirt pocket and felt a little calmer. The cell phone was tucked inside. She could call for help if she needed it.

Rachel knew she should have told her parents. She knew she should have called Will's dad, and she knew she should have called the police. But, they would ask too many questions. They would slow everything down and there was no time. She had to find Will.

Just a short time before, Rachel had made this same ride. Then, even though she was scared, she had thought she had everything under control. All she had to do was put the coins back and Will would be released. Now, everything had changed. Now, she no longer had what the kidnapper wanted.

Now, she was terrified.

As Rachel rode, she planned. She could pretend to bury a coin at midnight and wait for the kidnapper to show. Then she would tackle the kidnapper and make her tell where Will was. But, the stretch of beach was too big for her to catch the person who picked up the coin. In order to not be seen, she would have to wait too far away. There was no place to hide on an open sandy beach. The kidnapper could easily wait to be sure no one was around. Then the kidnapper could run to the spot, grab the coin, and run away. But, when the kidnapper realized the coin she demanded was not there—Rachel didn't let herself think about that. She had to find Will.

Rachel left her bike at the side of the path and walked to the front entrance of the hotel. Perhaps, if she stayed calm, she could find some answers. She knew the kidnappers had lured Will to the Isles View Hotel. Maybe she could find out what happened to him.

Rachel had ruled Barb out as a suspect. Barb was a blond, but had short hair. The first figure had long hair. And the second figure, although wearing a hooded jacket of some kind, was thinner, she was sure, than Barb, and she moved faster than Rachel thought Barb was capable of moving. That left Hat Lady. And if it was Hat Lady, Khaki Man would be a problem.

Rachel entered the lobby of the hotel just as Barb Simmons

came around the corner carrying a set of towels. She looked startled when she saw Rachel. "What are you doing here this time of night?"

Rachel took a deep breath and answered as calmly as possible. "I'm looking for Will."

"Will? Why would you think Will was here?" She waited for an answer from Rachel. When an answer didn't come she asked, "Do you know what time it is?"

"Have you seen him?" Rachel asked. "I think he was here earlier."

Barb set the towels down on the lobby counter. "Honey, you don't look very good. Is everything okay?"

"Yeah, everything's fine." Rachel tried to sound nonchalant. "I'm supposed to meet Will here."

Barb gave Rachel a puzzled look. "At this time of night?"

Rachel stuck with her story. "Yes, have you seen him?"

"Well, I haven't seen him, but let me ask Ben. He's in the residence."

Rachel walked to the lobby windows that faced the parking lot. A light by the building shone brightly, lighting up the walkway but not the sandy beach. In fact, it was so bright right outside the window, it contrasted to the darkness on the beach. It would be next to impossible to see anything out on the sand from anywhere close to this side of the building.

The only way to get to the beach was along the hotel walkway, or through the bushes where Rachel had hidden, unless someone climbed over the rocks at either end of the private beach. But that would be risky-going even during the daylight. The rocks were high, unstable and sharp. In the dark, it would be virtually impossible. But, if they came through the back of the hotel...

"Rachel?" Ben Simmons startled her. "Barb said you're looking for Will." Ben didn't look happy. "What's going on?"

Rachel looked up at the wall behind the check-in counter. There wasn't much time.

She said, "I think Will was here earlier, so I thought maybe he left me a message."

Ben's look softened. "Is everything alright?"

Rachel wondered if she was wearing a sign that said something was wrong. She ignored his question and asked one of her own. "Did he leave a message?"

"He was here earlier. He picked up the note you left him on the counter."

"The note on the counter?"

Ben nodded. "There was an envelope addressed to him on the counter. I assumed it was from you."

Rachel didn't respond. The kidnapper had called Will's house, left a message for Will to meet her at the Isles View

Hotel, and then left a note for him. Mr. Reynolds took the message, so Will would not have had any way to know it wasn't Rachel on the phone. But the note. Will should have recognized the handwriting unless, like the note left on her door, it was printed. Or perhaps it was typed.

Ben asked again, "Rachel, are you sure everything is okay?"

Rachel's head throbbed. She wanted to tell Ben, but she didn't know how he could help. He would call the police and she needed to find Will. "*No Police!*" the caller had demanded.

Rachel didn't answer him, but asked, "Did he say where he was going? Do you know which way he went?"

"No." Ben looked at her skeptically, but said nothing more.

"Thanks," Rachel mumbled as she moved quickly through the lobby to the back door. Maybe Will left something outside that would provide a clue. Rachel stepped out the back door and closed it behind her. It was pitch-black outside, now. Rachel heard the pounding of the surf.

Chapter Sixteen

A sliver of moonlight lit the sand as Rachel walked slowly toward the rock formation. She hoped the kidnapper was watching her. It was critical the kidnapper believe Rachel was delivering the missing coin. She felt a chill even though the air temperature was warm.

When she reached the rocks, Rachel bent down and placed a dime on the sand. She didn't know which coin was supposedly missing, but both were silver. This time she looked up at the windows of the Isles View Hotel to see if anyone was watching her. Most of the lights were off. It was almost midnight. Most of the hotel guests would be sound asleep. There was light coming from the right, third-floor unit, but Rachel could see that the drapes were pulled shut. If anyone was watching, it was from one of the darkened rooms.

She stood and looked up and down the beach. It appeared deserted, but it was impossible to tell for sure. The moonlight was dim and shone down in a narrow streak. Rachel could only see about 20 feet in any direction in the darkness.

She walked slowly back toward the hotel and along the path that led to the parking lot. She pretended to walk back to the road, but ducked into some sea rose bushes and doubled back to the hotel. She crept along the outside of the building and waited by the hotel's back door. It was still black where she stood. Rachel knew no one would be able to see her in the darkness. From here, she might be able to get to the kidnapper before she ran away. It was her only chance.

She checked her watch. The dial was illuminated just enough to see that it was 11:58. The last time she had placed the coins back at the rock formation, the kidnapper had come right away. Rachel hoped this time would be the same. She leaned against the building and crossed her arms over her chest. She could feel her heart pounding.

She heard the back doorknob turn and pressed herself against the wall as tightly as she could. The door opened slightly casting a faint light over the area. Rachel believed the light was coming from the lobby. It was dim and she knew it wasn't likely anyone could see her, but she inched away from it. Then the door closed. Rachel could feel the panic start to well inside her. Was that the kidnapper? Had she been seen? Had she ruined her chance to help Will? Should she try to go through the door after the person?

The doorknob turned again. This time the door swung open and the light was brighter. A figure stepped outside and Rachel immediately recognized Barb. Rachel lunged away from the light and landed with a thud on the sand.

"Who's there?" Barb demanded.

Rachel took off running. She couldn't risk being seen. Barb would ask too many questions. She thrashed through the bushes, scratching her legs. When she was a safe distance away, Rachel looked back. Barb had tightened or replaced the light bulb by the back door. Now, bright light illuminated the area. She couldn't go back to wait there.

Rachel's eyes suddenly caught sight of a figure standing outside, close to the downstairs suite rented by Khaki Man and Hat Lady. Rachel crouched down immediately to be sure no one could see her.

Because the light by the back door had been out earlier, Rachel had not been able to see down to the rock formation. Now, it was much brighter. Now, the kidnapper would be visible. Rachel's heart began to beat even faster. What if the kidnapper gave up, knowing she might be seen? Then how would she find Will?

Rachel watched the figure lurking by the downstairs suite when the back door of the main hotel suddenly opened and the light by the back door went out again. It happened so quickly Rachel had not been able to see who doused the light. She tried to adjust her eyes and look out toward the rock formation. She caught just a glimpse of someone running to the rocks. Watching, Rachel was quite certain it was a female. The figure was halfway there and Rachel made her move.

She was farther away this time than she had hoped. Having to move away from the hotel because Barb had tightened the light had pulled her out of position. The figure had already reached the rocks when Rachel cleared the bushes. She stumbled, but scrambled to her feet and took off running toward the figure at full speed, but the figure was halfway across the sand running back toward the hotel parking area.

Rachel now saw two other figures on the beach. As she got closer, she recognized them. Khaki Man was coming from the far side of the rocks and Hat Lady from the near side. *They* were running after the figure, too!

The figure was in front of all of them and moving too fast. They weren't going to catch up. Rachel screamed, "*Stop!*" The figure continued running, right through the dark side of the parking lot. Rachel cleared the sand and continued after the fleeing thief when suddenly light flooded the area. Rachel threw her hands up to shield her eyes.

"Everybody Freeze!" A voice shouted through a megaphone.

Rachel stopped dead in her tracks and squinted through the brightness. Next to her, Khaki Man and Hat Lady did the same.

Directly in front of them, the figure stopped, too. Rachel could only see her back. She was sure it was a female wearing jeans and a dark sweatshirt with the hood pulled up.

From the darkness a large man stepped into the light. It was Officer Landry, a veteran police officer on the Olde Locke Beach police force. "Nobody move," he directed. "The place is surrounded."

"That's her! That's the thief! That's the kidnapper!" Rachel blurted out, pointing to the hooded person in front of her.

Other police officers stepped out into the light and Officer Landry directed, "Everybody stay calm. We're going to break you up and ask you a few questions. The hotel owners called us about a problem, and I also received calls from both the Reynolds and Clark families about their missing children."

"But, she knows where Will is!" Rachel shouted again. "She kidnapped Will!"

A female police officer walked toward Rachel motioning with her hand for Rachel to step to the right, away from the group. Rachel lunged forward and pulled the hood from the figure's head. Rachel expected to see long blond hair tumble down, but she didn't. The hair was dark.

The figure turned around and glared at Rachel. She hissed in a whisper that only Rachel could hear, "You stupid little girl! All you had to do is give me all of the coins!"

Rachel whispered back, "I did."

"Liar!" She then threw herself at Rachel and shouted for all to hear, "She stole my coins!"

Officer Landry stepped between them and grabbed the girl's arms. Rachel screamed back at her, "Where's Will?" She turned to Officer Landry and pleaded, "She's got Will! She has to tell us where Will is!"

Rachel stared at the girl. She was about fifteen or sixteen and looked vaguely familiar. The girl shouted, "She has the stolen coin!" She pointed at Rachel.

Rachel's mouth went dry. She didn't have any stolen coins. She didn't have any coins at all. Rachel looked at Officer Landry. "Stolen?"

Officer Landry let go of the girl's arm. He turned and faced Rachel. "Do you have the coins?"

"No," Rachel stammered, "Well...uh yes...I mean...no." She could feel a wave of panic coming over her. How could she make anyone understand what happened when she didn't know what happened herself? If she didn't make Officer

Landry understand, what would happen to Will? And who was this girl? Why did she look so familiar?

Officer Landry moved forward and now took Rachel's arm. The girl started to walk away. "No!" Rachel blurted out.

Officer Landry signaled three other officers. "Nobody is going anywhere." Within moments the officers had separated Rachel, the girl, Khaki Man, and Hat Lady. Rachel heard Officer Landry say, "Find that girl's parents."

Officer Landry walked Rachel over to the back door of the hotel. Rachel pleaded once again, "She kidnapped Will!" Rachel blurted out the story as fast as she could. There was no time to waste. Officer Landry listened silently until she finished.

"Rachel, that's quite a story."

"It's true! I…"

She was cut off by one of the officers who walked over to join them. "Alex," the officer said, "I think you'd better hear what these folks have to say." Khaki Man and Hat Lady stood behind him.

Rachel felt another rush of adrenaline. They may be in on it with the girl, Rachel worried. She started to explain, "They've been following…"

Officer Landry held up his hand for her to be silent, but she couldn't stop herself, "They've been following us for the…"

Officer Landry gave her a stern look. "If you insist upon talking, I'll have one of the officers escort you to a patrol car and you can wait for me there."

This time Rachel was silent. She didn't want to wait in a patrol car. She needed to hear what Khaki Man and Hat Lady had to say. In the background she could hear the girl complaining that she wanted her mother.

Rachel glared at Khaki Man and Hat Lady. Hat Lady met her eyes, and then looked down. Rachel saw that Hat Lady's hands were trembling.

"We're coin collectors," Hat Lady began. "Someone stole four of our coins the first night we were here."

Khaki Man spoke, "We thought it was this girl and that boy she was with."

"Will," Rachel told him. "His name is Will." She looked from Khaki Man to Hat Lady. "Where is he? Do you know where he is?"

They both shook their heads no.

Hat Lady continued, directing her words to Rachel, "We went to the police as soon as we discovered the theft."

Officer Landry nodded.

"We even told the police we thought you and that boy, I mean Will, were the ones who stole the coins."

"Us?" Rachel was stunned. "Why would you think that?"

Khaki Man answered, "Well, you did have the coins, right?"

"But, I found them on the beach, over by those rocks." Rachel pointed to the rock formation.

Hat Lady added, "The police said they didn't believe it was you and the boy. Even the hotel owners, Barb and Ben, backed you up."

Rachel was relieved momentarily. At least the police and Ben and Barb didn't believe she and Will were guilty of the theft of the coins. She asked, "How did you know we had the coins?"

Khaki Man answered, "We didn't at first. You were just acting so suspicious and nosing around. We started to think you were planning on trying to steal more of our coins. Especially after I caught you peeking into our window today."

Rachel glanced up at Officer Landry and smiled weakly.

Hat Lady now spoke. "So, we started to set a trap for you." "But," Khaki Man interrupted her, "when your friend showed up, he seemed confused by a note left on the hotel desk. So, we started to wonder."

Hat Lady continued the story, "We decided to watch you and the boy, but we haven't seen him since he walked out of the hotel. We saw you out on the beach by the rocks earlier."

Khaki Man jumped in again. "We were beginning to believe you and Will were victims, but weren't sure until you came around asking questions tonight. We were in the room by the lobby and overheard. That's when we followed you and waited in the rocks."

Suddenly, a loud voice came out of nowhere startling everyone. Even Officer Landry jumped.

"It was her!" the voice shouted. "She stole the coins!" The figure with the angry voice stood on the sand and pointed at the girl with the hooded sweatshirt. Standing with the figure was a female police officer.

"Will!" Rachel shouted. "It's you." Her voice caught with emotion as she ran to him, "I thought something awful had happened to you." Rachel reached out and embraced him in a big hug. She fought back tears. "I'm so glad you're okay."

Rachel stepped away from him. He hadn't returned the hug. Will looked angry and hurt. He accused, "I can't believe you didn't give her both of the coins!"

"What?" Rachel replied. "Wait a minute!" It suddenly came to her. Will thought she had held back a coin. "Will, I did! I left both the coins."

He glared at her and then pushed past her. Will walked over to Officer Landry. The female officer followed, explaining, "I found him locked in a storage shed over there." She gestured toward the gardening shed. "He was locked in a shed behind that one."

Rachel ran behind Will frantically calling, "Will, you've got to believe me!"

Will didn't pay any attention to her, but spoke to Officer Landry. He repeated, "It was her!" He pointed at the girl again.

The girl from the beach was wide-eyed as she looked at Will.

"Wait," Will now pointed at Rachel and glared, "she may still have one of the other coins."

Rachel thought she might get sick. She wasn't sure if it was because the police might now think she stole a coin, or whether it was because Will thought so. How could he think she would risk his life for a lousy coin? Words flew out of her mouth as she shoved Will to the ground, "You stupid dope! How could you possibly think I would do that to you?"

Officer Landry, Khaki Man, and Hat Lady all stared at Rachel with their mouths open.

Will tried to get to his feet, but she shoved him down again. "Dope! Dope! Dope!"

Officer Landry stepped forward to stop her. "Wait a minute!" he said to Rachel as she stood over Will, her hands braced against her hips.

"Alright already!" Will said. "I believe you!" He looked up at her. "Is it okay if I get up, or are you going to push me down again?"

Rachel stood her ground. She had every right to be angry, she thought. How could Will have believed she would do such a thing. She had been so worried.

Officer Landry chuckled as he extended a hand to Will.

Will took it and stood up. "I've been locked in a shed on the other side of the garden shed." He shivered slightly. "It was full of spiders. I hate spiders!" Will then pointed to the girl with the hooded sweatshirt. "She locked me in."

The girl shouted back, "You're crazy!"

Will continued, "I got a phone message from Rachel. Well, I thought it was from Rachel. She said to meet her at the hotel." Will looked over at Rachel.

"I didn't call you," Rachel declared.

"Okay!" he said, and continued the story. "When I got here, there was a note in an envelope signed 'R'. It said to go behind the gardening shed. When I did, someone pushed me into the shed and shoved something between the shed door handles and I couldn't get out."

"Did you know who pushed you?" Officer Landry asked.

"Not when it happened." He turned to Rachel and explained, "It was like when two of the coins were stolen from us at the beach."

Rachel nodded.

"So," Officer Landry pressed him, "How do you know *that*

young lady was responsible?"

He gestured toward the girl who once again took the opportunity to say, "Liar!"

Officer Landry directed another officer, "Get her further away."

Will continued, "She didn't say anything at first. She just left me stuck in there. I tried yelling for help and banging on the side of the shed, but the ocean surf was too loud and I gave up."

Officer Landry asked again, "So, how do you know it was her?"

"After Rachel left one of the coins instead of two…"

"I left two!" Rachel interjected.

Will ignored her and continued, "That girl came to me at the shed and told me that my girlfriend had done me in. That she ran off with one of the coins." Will turned red immediately. He looked at Rachel. "That's what she said."

"I left two coins," Rachel reiterated.

Will kept talking, "She disguised her voice, but I saw her through a small gap between the shed doors. It was her."

"Are you positive?" Officer Landry asked.

Will nodded, but added, "There was enough moonlight to see her clearly, but she didn't know it." Will shook his head. "I was so mad at Rachel, I started talking to her. And she was so mad at Rachel that she told me the whole story."

Will now spoke to Rachel, "Her family is staying here at the Isles View Hotel. She and her sister stole the coins from one of the rooms and then buried them in the sand. They were going to tell their mother they found the coins, but we found them before they came back."

Rachel exclaimed, "That's who she is! I knew she looked familiar! She and her sister were leaving the beach when Greta and I arrived. They really didn't want to go and now I know why!"

Will nodded. "She admitted to everything. She told me she followed you the other night. She left the note on your door, too, and she hit me over the head while her sister held the bathroom door shut, trapping you inside. They had seen me with the pouch and thought all the coins were inside it."

"So she and her sister stole the two coins from us on the boardwalk that night and now wanted the other two?"

"She was really mad when you left only one coin tonight."

Rachel flared again. "I left two…"

Will held up his hands. "I believe you, but where's the other coin?"

Officer Landry looked confused. "What do you mean, the first time?"

Rachel explained how she had made two trips to deliver the coins to the spot where she and Will had found them.

"But after I left the coins the first time, someone went over to the rocks!" Rachel turned and looked at everyone. "I saw her. Well, sort of, but it wasn't that girl. It was definitely not that girl."

Khaki Man and Hat Lady looked at each other and then at Rachel. Hat Lady said, "She came right after you placed the coins by the rock—dressed in white with long blond hair."

"You saw her?" Rachel exclaimed. "I wasn't sure if I was seeing things!"

"I saw her," Hat Lady said. She looked uncomfortably over at Khaki Man. "It was as if she came out of nowhere."

Khaki Man nodded. "She disappeared as quickly as she came. Then, that girl came." He pointed to the girl in the hooded sweatshirt.

"Alex," an officer walked up to Officer Landry. "The girl's mother is here."

Rachel watched the woman approach. She recognized her, and standing in the background was another girl. "That's the sister," Rachel told them. "I saw her the day we found the coins."

The girl with the blond hair stood, partially obscured by her mother's shadow.

Rachel looked at Khaki Man, who looked at Hat Lady, who looked back at Rachel. They all stood in silence. Rachel knew they were all thinking the same thing. Was she the figure with the blond hair? Did she steal the first coin?

The officer said to Officer Landry, "The mother wants to talk to you."

"Will you make a statement about what you told me?" Officer Landry asked Will.

"With pleasure," Will replied.

"Wait here." Officer Landry walked a short distance away.

Khaki Man said to Hat Lady, "Is she the one who arrived first?" He didn't sound certain.

"I don't know," she answered.

Rachel grabbed Will's sweatshirt sleeve and pulled him to one side. "Will, remember that I told you I saw a figure by the rocks just before finding the coins?"

"Yeah," he said. "You saw yellow, which could be the sister's blond hair—and you saw white. She could have been dressed in white." Will then concluded, "So you saw the sister by the rocks just before you found the coins."

Rachel shook her head. "No, that's impossible. That girl over there with the blond hair left the beach with her sister and mother just as I arrived with Greta. She didn't come back until I was leaving the beach." Rachel looked directly into Will's eyes. "It's impossible. She couldn't be the one I saw by the rocks when I found the coins."

"But," Will said, "you never really got a good look that day. You weren't even sure you saw someone."

"That's true," Rachel admitted.

"And," Will continued, "that doesn't matter. It could still be the blond sister who took one of the coins tonight."

Rachel was still bewildered. "Did you really believe the dark-haired girl thought I left only one coin? Could she have been lying?"

"No." Will was certain. "She was definitely mad. She really believed you held back a coin."

Rachel tensed. "If the blond sister picked it up, why didn't the other sister know?"

Will raised his eyebrows and said, "Who knows? Maybe she was holding out on her sister."

Rachel looked over at Officer Landry. He was talking with the mother of the two girls. "Will," she asked him, "did the girl tell you which coin was missing? I had two coins. I had the French coin, dated later than when the pirates were here, and I had the coin from 1708. That coin clearly could have belonged to..." She didn't finish the sentence.

Will looked uncomfortable. "The missing coin was the silver one from 1708," he told her.

Rachel gazed out over the Atlantic Ocean toward the Isles of Shoals. The islands were invisible in the darkness. Was it possible that the ghost of Blackbeard's wife took the 1708 coin? No, it wasn't possible, she thought. Absolutely impossible! Or was it?

Chapter Seventeen

Rachel teetered, with both heels on the curb and her toes extending over the edge, as Will loaded his bag into the back-seat of the car. Rachel glanced at the bag. "Shorts and tee shirts?"

Will pressed his lips together and nodded. "And my bathing suit for the pool at Mom's apartment."

Rachel teetered too far and fell off. "A pool, huh?"

"Yeah," Will said. "Mom says the beach is about ten miles away from where she lives."

Now Rachel smiled. "Well, a pool's okay."

Will smiled, too. "The beach is better."

Will pulled the coin out of his pocket that Khaki Man and Hat Lady had given them as a reward. They had felt so bad about accusing Rachel and Will of theft, they had given them a coin from their collection. "Here, you hang on to it," he said.

"Really?" Rachel asked. "It's your turn for this month."

Will handed her the coin. " I promised I wouldn't take any of our coins to California, remember? Besides, this way you'll know I'm coming back soon." He grinned at her. "There's no way I'm letting you hang on to it for too long!"

"That's right!" she said. "And I'm not sending it to you. You'll have to come back to get it." She put the coin into her pocket.

"You know, the police never did find the missing 1708 coin," Will said. "I talked with Officer Landry yesterday and he said the girls admitted to everything that happened, but denied ever having the last coin." He moved closer to Rachel and added, "It's a good thing I trust you. Those girls still say you pocketed the coin."

Rachel felt a wave of guilt, but knew she hadn't done anything wrong. "It's weird that they wouldn't admit to having the coin if they admitted to everything else." She hesitated. "That coin was dated 1708. It was the closest in date to the time Blackbeard and The Scot were here, so it could have been..." She still couldn't say it out loud.

Will nodded. "I was thinking the same thing, but we can't be certain the blond sister didn't keep a coin for herself." He was just about to say something else when Mr. Reynolds came out the front door and walked toward them. He nodded to Rachel. "Will, we need to get going. Logan Airport is going to be busy and we need to check in two hours before your flight."

Rachel and Will looked at each other awkwardly. Then Rachel said, "I'll make reservations at the café for the day you come back. We'll have pizza and root beer."

Will grinned at her. "Deal." Then he climbed into the car and shut the door.

Mr. Reynolds went to the driver's side and looked over at Rachel. For a moment, she thought he looked as upset about Will leaving as she was. He didn't speak. He nodded to her again, slid into the driver's seat and closed the door.

As the car pulled away from the curb, Rachel waved. Then she reached into her pocket and wrapped her fingers around the coin Will had just given her. She said aloud, "You will come back. You will come back. You will come back."
